An Old Shrew, A Tortured Soul, And Everyday Angels

ROSINA ANDERSON

PAGE PUBLISHING, INC.
Conneaut Lake, PA

First originally published by Page Publishing 2020

ISBN 978-1-64628-746-8 (pbk)
ISBN 978-1-64628-747-5 (digital)

Printed in the United States of America

CHAPTER

Early one morning, Olga stepped out onto her third-floor balcony, took a deep breath of fresh air, and looked down on the park adjacent to her building. Startled by her sudden appearance, a blackbird sitting on the rooftop, welcoming the first rays of the sun with its sweet song, spread its wings to search for a safer perch on a blooming red chestnut tree some distance away.

What a beautiful spot this is at daybreak, reflected Olga. No human voices to disturb the peace, no noisy children or men and women hurrying to and fro in animated conversation. No one to bother her. Not yet. It was too early for them, which made Olga feel blissfully alone and in sole charge of the world.

From the north side of the park where she lived, Olga could see the roofs of some of the summer cottages scattered throughout the community garden on the south side. Originally these small wooden structures were meant to serve as places for the tenants of the plots to store their tools, have an occasional meal, and enjoy their music while working in their gardens on the weekends.

But World War II had changed all that. When the conflict had finally ended, Bavaria and specifically Olga's hometown had been obligated to take in a large number of displaced persons who, driven from their homes, had nowhere else to go. With so many dwellings in ruins and, therefore, a dearth of places where they could be housed, the local government had decided to allot these cottages to them until better accommodations could be found. This, however, had never happened, and the cottages had become permanent shelters to a very interesting conglomerate of characters. It was a poor but happy place.

Thinking of the refugees who occupied it, Olga realized she did not care for them at all. What did their concerns matter to her? She was now over eighty years old, had lived through the war and gotten through life without anyone's help. So why should these people get public assistance, she asked herself. What had they ever done to deserve it? Did they think they could just invade her country and take food out of the mouths of tax-paying citizens? If her hometown allowed this to happen, it was going to pot.

Every time she thought about the unfairness of it all, Olga worked herself into a rage. She turned around, went back inside, and slammed the balcony door with such force that the window panes rattled and her pet, a brownish-pink Maltese terrier named Fluffy, cried out in protest. "Sorry I startled you," Olga apologized. "But I don't like these foreigners." And it occurred to her that, regardless of nationality, there were not too many people she did like. The only living creature that she really cared about besides herself was Fluffy who was purebred, of course, as for Olga a simple mutt or rescue dog would not have been good enough. Olga was so proud of his perfect lineage that she displayed a stack of impressive papers documenting it on a little stand by her door, ready to show it off to the select few who were allowed to cross her threshold.

Fluffy was spoiled. He slept at the foot of Olga's bed and ate only the best cuts of meat that Olga chose for him most carefully at the butcher shop. No cheap or ready-made dog food for him! Whenever she took him to the park, he wore a colorful outfit especially knitted or crocheted for him by Olga's neighbor Hilde in hopes of one day inheriting Olga's home. For Olga was the only one in the building who, when the flats came up for sale, had the funds to buy hers. Everyone else was still renting.

Hilde was not the only neighbor who had been promised Olga's home upon her death. Quite a few other ladies, too, had been made the same promise. They all tried to stay on Olga's good side, do chores for her, and appease her at every turn so as not to be left out of her will. In reality Olga had other ideas: While she enjoyed taking advantage of her neighbors, her home had been earmarked for an animal charity.

If the neighbors had sat down together to have a serious talk about Olga, they might have found out how devious she really was and that she was only using them to make her own life easier. Such a conversation, however, never took place, and Olga's promise was never mentioned, not even among close friends, because every single one of them was too embarrassed to admit that she was after Olga's flat, a fact that was not lost on Olga and on which she knew she could count. So they were all left in the dark as to Olga's real motives, and each remained convinced that she was Olga's favorite, personally chosen by her to receive the best gift she could bestow upon her death: a home that was completely paid for, the only home her heir would ever own.

Olga was not just devious, she was vain to her fingertips. She fancied herself a woman of impeccable birth and breeding and habitually scrutinized others from the tops of their heads to the soles of their feet, always finding something to criticize. Desperate to be admired not only for her appearance but also her achievements, she claimed credit for making Fluffy's fun outfits when people commented on their beauty. With deep satisfaction, she accepted their compliments, always fishing for more, although being recognized for her looks would have meant more to her than being acknowledged for such menial skills as Hilde's knitting and crocheting.

Olga found herself hugely attractive. Every morning she posed and primped in front of the mirror, adjusting her dowdy bob of reddish-brown chin-length hair which she amateurishly cut and dyed herself, not just because she was stingy—which she certainly was—but also because she felt she could do a much better job than any lowly beautician. In her opinion, hairdressers were not worth a flip, not that she herself achieved miraculous results: Her hair was uneven in length and color and far from stylish, her simple coiffure having remained unchanged for two or three decades.

After arranging her hair, Olga took a pained look at her mottled complexion, quickly covered it with talcum powder, and then inspected her yellowish teeth which, to her profound regret, she had been told could not be whitened. In the end, their color did not matter since she hardly ever laughed, and no one noticed. What others did observe were her piercing brown eyes that did not miss anything, her small pouting mouth, and her lips pursed in displeasure, all overshadowing her one redeeming feature: the shape of her face. It was a perfect heart which could have been pleasing, had her expression been less sour.

Olga was short and stocky, and her clothes, expensive when bought years ago, were still in relatively good condition but no longer fashionable. She usually wore jackets and skirts with matching blouses and donned dresses for special occasions but would not be caught dead in unladylike pants. To flaunt her "elegant" legs, she preferred high heels over ordinary flats which she disliked intensely and put aside exclusively for days of mud and snow. In the winter, she loved to parade her fur coats, invariably sending pungent whiffs of moth balls into the air.

Before going out, she applied a bright scarlet lipstick, often leaving smudges of it on her teeth. She then unfailingly and obsessively checked for lint on her clothes, the tiniest mote of which, to her, would have been an intolerable blemish. When she finally exited her flat, she was bedecked with one of her signature hats made of felt, with at least one magnificent feather jutting out on top.

Olga was so fixated on lint that she had the irritating habit of looking for it on everyone she came across. When she did make out a minute speck of it, she tutted loudly and waggled her forefinger at the offender. She then picked it off as if it were a slimy flea, hair, or spider, and as she then demonstratively and daintily held it up to the person's face, her put-on shudder turned into a triumphant smirk.

No one was too happy to come across Olga in the park where they were walking their dogs. She could be spotted from afar, her head held high, and her body so straight that it looked like she had swallowed a stick. As soon as people saw her coming, they grabbed their own pets and ran for the hills, hoping to get away unnoticed. But most of the time it was too late. Olga's beady eyes were sharp, and causing trouble amused her. So she called them back with a voice so shrill that it carried throughout the park and seriously embarrassed them, leaving them no choice but to face her.

In the event that they were stubborn and kept going anyway, she delighted in following them until they could no longer ignore her, which often resulted in a dreaded encounter between the pets. Whenever a dog dared to approach, or, heaven forbid, go so far as to growl at Fluffy, there was war. Olga could not contain herself and the loudest arguments ensued, accompanied by furious barking on both sides, and when the fighting parties had finally exhausted their strength and endurance, tough Olga generally had the last word.

CHAPTER

But not always. It so happened one late afternoon that, following an especially fierce exchange, Olga accidentally let go of Fluffy's leash, and he, free for once, shot off toward the nearby Cemetery of the Church of Peace, with Olga in desperate pursuit. Her handbag was flapping, her hat fell off, and she kept tripping on her high heels. In spite of her efforts, she could not reach Fluffy, and all her appeals to the bystanders to help her get hold of him fell on deaf ears. They were too busy laughing at "poor" Olga, happy that for once karma had caught up with her.

For her, worse was yet to come. While chasing after Fluffy inside the cemetery, Olga failed to realize that it was getting later and later until it was time for the attendant to make his rounds and ring his bell to alert any visitors to the fact that he was about to lock the gates. In all the excitement, Olga either did not hear, or paid no attention to the bell. When she finally found Fluffy sitting on her family's grave, she grabbed his leash and turned to leave but, to her horror, found herself locked in.

Exasperated, she looked up to the spikes on top of the ornate wrought-iron gates and the shards of glass that surmounted the six-foot high walls and realized to her dismay that there was no way she could scale them. With the sun going down, any chance of her getting out was fading. Had she been more sensitive, she would have been in tears. But not resolute and feisty Olga. "Help," she kept screaming at the top of her lungs until she eventually attracted the attention of a man and his adult son who, like her, were visitors to the cemetery and now equally locked in.

After several futile attempts, the father, careful not to tear his clothes, eventually managed to climb over the wall. His son then hoisted first Fluffy and then Olga up to the top where Olga stood shuddering and wobbling among the sharp pieces of glass until she summoned up the courage to let herself go and be caught by the older man on the other side. They were soon joined by the son who had easily mounted and jumped off the wall.

Did Olga thank them for their good deed? Of course not. Instead she sniveled over a scratch on her hand and a rip in her skirt.

Olga would have loved to forget about this humiliating incident but was to be reminded of it by an article which appeared in the paper a day or two later. Submitted by her rescuers and entitled "Imprisoned in the Cemetery," it reported the unfortunate episode in detail and shockingly referred to her by name. Olga stared at it in disbelief. She was absolutely mortified, knowing that everyone else had read it, too, and, while she was agonizing over the feasibility of suing the editors, her fellow citizens were having a good laugh at her expense whenever they caught a glimpse of her on the street.

Olga cringed at the memory of it. Why did it have to happen to her? For once the tables were turned, and Olga who loved to gossip about others and had no compunctions about spreading malicious rumors was now made fun of and talked about herself. What misery! Her pride was crushed, and there was no place for her to hide. All she saw was gloating faces. Even the children were pointing their fingers at her and giggling at her misfortune.

CHAPTER

Zora, too, could not suppress a smile at Olga's predicament although she was perhaps the most understanding. For she knew what it felt like to be the target of people's contempt and ridicule—not because she was bad-tempered and cynical like Olga—but because of her heritage. Her parents were Gypsies who perished in a concentration camp from which Zora was the only one in her family to escape. She now occupied one of the cottages in the community garden.

About sixty years old, she was short and striking. Her big black eyes animated her soft round face and were always dancing and sparkling with pleasure and gaiety. She usually wore a colorful flowered shawl which covered both her dark hair and the shoulders of her simple dress. Her happy laughter brightened her neighbors' day, and sometimes they sat spell-bound as, on her tiny porch, she sang traditional songs in the language of her ancestors, her uniquely beautiful voice ringing out over the park and bringing tears to their eyes.

Everyone loved her. She was easygoing and kind, and her door was always open. She made everyone feel welcome with a friendly greeting and a twinkle in her eyes. Her generosity knew no bounds. She shared the flowers, vegetables, and herbs she grew on her small plot of land with her neighbors and freely offered ointments and other remedies she had made from her plants to those who needed them. She had a great deal of common sense, a highly developed intuition, and a quick and astute perception, and her advice was valued by all. She was the only one fully capable of seeing through Olga's façade and, on occasion, was known to discreetly warn a neighbor of her duplicity.

Like Olga, Zora, too, had a pet but an unconventional and undemanding one: a black crow named Max who usually sat on the porch rails or the window ledge and whose funny antics never failed to make her laugh. In the early morning hours, he woke her up with his caws and, during the day, presented her with all sorts of glittering objects he found in the park. He was a wonderful listener and occasionally surprised Zora with a silly expression he had picked up from his other human friends, especially the children.

Zora talked to Max about her secret dreams of one year taking part in a pilgrimage to Saintes-Maries-de-la-Mer in Provence where Gypsies unite to pay homage to their patron saint, Sara la Kali or Black Sara. A picture of this saint which adorned her wall was a prized possession rescued from her parents' home, together with a chain on which blue glass beads resembling eyes were strung to shield her from harm. The gold coin she was given at birth had been stolen.

In spite of a lengthy investigation, the perpetrator of this theft had never been determined although initially there were two strong suspects: Adi, Zora's next-door neighbor in the community garden, and Fabian, the third child of an affluent family residing in a big house at the west end of the park. Adi, initially regarded as possibly culpable on the basis of his proximity, was tentatively ruled out, however, when all who knew him vouched for his innocence.

CHAPTER

4

As an infant, Adi had been found crying and starving in the arms of his mother who, along with her husband, had perished on their grueling trek from Poland to the West after the war. Like so many of their compatriots, they had left all their belongings behind and risked their lives to flee their homes in desperate fear of the atrocities widely attributed to the advancing Soviet forces.

On their way to the safety of Allied-occupied Germany, they had hidden in deep forests, begged for food at countless strangers' doors, and braved the snow and bitter cold and ice of a harsh winter until they were chilled to the bone and weakened by hunger and disease. Unable to go on, they had finally given up their relentless struggle to find peace in death.

Wrapped in a warm blanket, only Adi had survived. He was taken to a displaced persons camp where everyone longed to hold the miracle baby who promised to brighten the bleakness of their days. They gathered around him and vowed never to allow anything to happen to him. The women who had lost their own children stepped up to take responsibility for his care, and the men played with him and made him giggle.

He again had a family, all of whom loved and adored him, and he returned their love with his first sweet smiles and a sunny disposition. As soon as he had learned to walk, he delighted in playing hide-and-seek, his funny little face and shock of red hair bobbing up and down behind the furniture. And whenever he was discovered, he filled the house with shrieks of joy.

Adi could not stand seeing sadness and tears and always tried to wipe them away. He climbed on the laps of those who looked troubled, put his arms around their necks, gently touched them with his tiny fingers, and with his soft big eyes gazed straight into their anguished ones, penetrating into their souls, melting their hearts, and dispelling their sorrow until it turned into laughter. He was their bright and shining light.

Since displaced persons camps were not meant to permanently house the multinational refugees from Eastern Europe as well as the former inmates of the Nazi concentration camps who had sought shelter there, Adi's family kept changing as some of its members moved out and a few new ones arrived. Those who left had to promise him to stay in touch, and they always did.

When Adi was almost six years old, the camp was scheduled to close, and Emil and Anetka, an older Polish couple, offered to take him with them to their allocated home, a small flat in the city, to give him a secure life, help him with school, and eventually see to his vocational training. Adi's foster father who was very handy with tools taught him basic carpentry while his foster mother instilled in him an appreciation of books and love of reading.

They were a happy family who loved each other until Emil succumbed to tuberculosis. Anetka whose health had never recovered from the inconceivable hardships she had endured during their trek to the West was so devastated by his death that she suffered a breakdown and had to be placed in a care facility. Adi, then of age, was moved from their flat to the summer house in the community garden where he became Zora's neighbor.

Anetka, of course, remained an important part of his life. She was the mother who had nurtured him and made many sacrifices for him for such a long time. He wanted her to feel cherished and, at least once a week, he took the bus to bring her flowers and her favorite chocolates. Seeing him regularly and sitting there quietly in his company made her happy and assured her of his continuing love and devotion until she, too, died a few years later.

Now a man in his forties, Adi was of slight build and delicate features, still instantly recognizable by the triangular tuft of red hair on top of his head. A happy-go-lucky soul, he always had a contagious smile on his face. He supplemented his meager income by working all sorts of odd jobs, and whatever he could spare, he shared with his neighbors who enjoyed having him around. He was upbeat and available whenever his help was needed. Incapable of hurting a fly, he would have been the last one to jeopardize his cordial relationship with Zora by stealing her possessions. They got along beautifully and traded jokes and laughter from their respective balconies every single day.

CHAPTER

Adi was soon officially cleared of all suspicion in the theft of Zora's coin. That left Fabian. This seventeen-year-old boy was the spoiled, arrogant, and devious brother to eighteen-year-old Monika, equally spoiled, arrogant, and devious, and nineteen-year-old Simon, of a slightly better disposition than his siblings. All three had been brought up in an upper middle class family with plenty of money to cater to their every whim. In their entire lives, no one had ever said no to them, neither their father Philipp, a geologist by profession, who used to take them all over the world, nor their mother Agnes, a former kindergarten and first grade teacher who dabbled in politics to enhance her prestige.

Their home was beautiful on the outside: a big two-story brick house built after the war and surrounded by a large fenced yard. The second floor was reserved exclusively for the children. It was their realm where they could do as they pleased. Their parents fully respected their privacy and left them alone unless an urgent matter came up, in which case they asked permission to enter.

The noise coming from upstairs did not seem to bother them although at times it was frightening. With nothing else to do and bored stiff because no one worked or went to school, Simon, Monika, and Fabian made it a game to destroy their home. Their second-story front door showed scars from changes of locks, carved initials, and cracks from all the kicks it had been subjected to. The paint looked old, worn, and faded. A naked light bulb in the hallway gave off a sickly glow. A dirty string hung from its socket which still held a sharp sliver of the original globe, the remaining fragments scattered on the filthy floor. The windows, too, were broken, and there were holes in the walls. Some of the furniture was in pieces, glass and porcelain lay shattered on torn carpeting, and graffiti defaced the ceilings.

No one had encouraged these young people to learn a trade or earn a living. None of them wanted or had to lift a finger, ever. They did no household chores of any kind—no cleaning, no cooking, no laundry—and whenever it occurred to them that they had run out of clean clothes, they simply threw their dirty outfits through an empty window frame or down the stairs for their mother to pick up and take care of. Agnes cooked all their meals for which the three siblings punctually showed up downstairs. There were no words of appreciation. They expected their mother's efforts and took them for granted. When they had finished eating, they simply tossed the dishes wherever they pleased, knowing that she would clean up after them without complaint. This callous behavior might have incensed other parents but Agnes saw absolutely nothing wrong with it and would have adamantly and fiercely defended it to an outsider. In her mind, love equated absolute tolerance, and by letting her children live their lives however they saw fit, she felt she was doing them the greatest favor of all.

Philipp and Agnes had recently separated, and since Philipp now lived miles away, he no longer had much influence on the children although he did care a great deal and provided for them generously. He was honest and upstanding and worked very hard, which did not leave him much time or the energy necessary to steer his family in a positive direction. With Philipp gone, there was no one left to curb Agnes's drinking which she now felt free to engage in more and more until, after each evening meal, she invariably disappeared into the basement where, among broken furniture, she kept an ample stash of red wine. She took two bottles and emptied them to the last drop. She then broke down crying and called Philipp at all hours of the night in a vain attempt to win him back.

That was the life Fabian was used to—doing whatever came to his mind and grabbing whatever he wanted, mostly at home but often elsewhere as well. Caught stealing repeatedly during his early teens, he remained a strong suspect in the disappearance of Zora's coin although no one was able to prove that he was the one to blame. There was a possibility that Monika, too, might have had a hand in it since she, like her brother, was known to have helped herself to things that did not belong to her.

Whereas Fabian was short and dumpy with unwashed slightly curly brown hair hanging to his shoulders, Monika had a sleek pink-dyed hairdo and was tall and skinny. Neither had any respect for others. They never smiled, hardly ever talked except with their peers, and seemed to be permanently pouting. Simon, blond, lean, long-limbed, and surpassing his sister in height, on the other hand, was friendly and polite to strangers but just as destructive as his siblings at home.

All three were lazy and utterly ungrateful for all that was provided for them. They felt entitled, and the words "thank you" and "please" were not part of their vocabulary. And yet, Agnes kept fulfilling their every wish. She bought their favorite clothes, prepared their favorite foods, and chauffeured them everywhere they felt like going, even out of town. Monika was the one who benefitted the most from the free rides as her mother drove her to the house of whichever boyfriend she had at the time, left her to spend the night, and picked her up whenever she was ready the next morning.

CHAPTER

A gnes, the proud mother of these "paragons of virtue," never once questioned the wisdom of her own permissiveness. Her children had the right to be totally free, and she had the obligation to see to it that they were. It was as simple as that. Anyone brave enough to intervene would have risked unleashing her fury. There was really nothing in Agnes's childhood or upbringing that would have accounted for her compulsive insistence on the total absence of any constraints or restrictions being placed on her children's lives. Agnes's own parents had been decent and well-educated people who adored her and her brother Toni. As most parents of their generation, they were fairly strict and established reasonable limits but always remained patient and kind.

While Toni stepped into the paternal mold, Agnes turned out to be a difficult and particularly willful child who learned early in life how to manipulate and outwit her elders and undermine the traditional values they stood for. She became sly and secretive and took to feeding her parents practically nothing but lies. The fact that these were rarely challenged prompted Agnes to mock her parents' simple-mindedness and gullibility. She disrespected everyone including her teachers, and as soon as she was legally old enough, escaped what she called the strait jacket of her home to run away and marry Philipp, her boyfriend at the time, without one word to her parents. Ironically, Phillip was to later become the single stabilizing force in her life.

Agnes, now in her early fifties, was bony and tall, with an angular chin, cold blue eyes, thin and firmly set lips, and straight sandy hair held in place by a pin. Once a promising artist, she had thrown away her talent, and what remained was a creature of falsehoods and deceit who blamed everyone but herself for what had gone wrong in her life and spread evil rumors about those who had the gall to criticize her. Her claws were out to wound her enemies, ready to strike with brown and deformed nails that looked like talons and immediately put people on their guard.

Her children's nefarious activities, of course, did not remain unnoticed. They greatly worried the neighbors who were afraid that their petty crimes might get out of hand and eventually jeopardize the safety, and disrupt the harmony, of the entire community. It was Olga who took charge of the situation. Just observing the siblings coming and going at all hours of the night had made them suspect in her eyes and aroused her indignation although, like everyone else, she was unaware of the destruction they had wreaked in Agnes's house. This cannot go on, she decided and, determined to take a stand, planned to discuss the wayward teens and their negligent mother with those neighbors in her building she considered worthy of her attention.

CHAPTER

There were only four. The rest were either "beneath" Olga, had not done enough for her, or had angered her in some way. The only ones favored by her at the moment were Hilde and Sylvia, both of whom lived on the second floor, and an older couple, Hans and his wife Frieda, who occupied a flat on the ground floor.

Hilde, the creator of Fluffy's wonderful outfits, had not experienced much joy in her life. Her parents had had no time for her and, growing up, she was always wondering whether she meant anything to them at all. She had the feeling she was barely tolerated and forever in their way. Maybe, she thought, they do love me but just can't show it. They never really talked to her which made her sad. She would have loved to tell them about her friends, the subjects she enjoyed in school, the places she would like to visit, her favorite meals, or what she wished for on her birthday. But they did not seem to be interested. Year after year, she was given the same presents: either a little glass or porcelain jar or a pair of socks. And the only toy she had ever received was an old doll from a trunk in the attic. It had a crack on its head and was missing its hair but Hilde loved it anyway.

In her teens, Hilde felt terribly alone, especially when she was falsely accused of having broken a mirror hanging in her aunt's bedroom. Why are they blaming me, Hilde wondered. She had never been in that room, and entering it would have been inconceivable as it had been hammered into her over and over from early childhood that bedrooms other than her own were off-limits. It was so unfair. Although innocent, she was promptly convicted and, from then on, regularly subjected to her parents' malicious innuendos concerning the incident. They would not let her forget it. On the contrary. They kept tormenting her with the memory of the injustice she had suffered, and, every time they loomed over her with the same allegation, all she could do was flinch and wipe away the tears that were rolling down her cheeks.

Equally cruel und hurtful were her parents' disparaging remarks about her "awkward gait" and "clumsiness" that were to haunt her into adulthood. They must be ashamed of me, she realized and was devastated. Desperate to elicit just one kind word once in a while, she made up her mind to be the best daughter she could possibly be. She was obedient and quiet, studied, and stayed out of her parents' way but, regardless of how hard she tried to be good, there was only criticism and coldness on their part, never giving Hilde a chance to find out what it felt like to be warm, cuddled, and loved.

Before Hilde had even completed her mandatory education, her parents, anxious to push her out of the house and make her go to work, had already made arrangements for her first job: laboring as a public lavatory attendant in a department store, which would be utterly demeaning and not pay but a pittance. Hilde would have preferred to learn a trade, and her parents could easily have afforded to continue supporting her but, as usual, no one was interested in her hopes and dreams, and she ended up doing as she was told. "How could they do this to me," she cried out. "It must be the worst job in the world, cleaning toilets all day long! How humiliating!" It was definitely not a job she could tell her friends about, and she was afraid one of them would eventually discover her in that unmentionable place.

After diligently working at the public lavatory for some time, Hilde could not tolerate the shame of it any longer and gave her notice. Subsequent jobs she held were more respectable but equally thankless until she was hired as a nurse's aide at a local hospital where, now in her mid to late fifties, she was a valued member of the staff.

To get away from her parents, Hilde had married when she was twenty-one. The few used pieces of furniture as well as the pretty vase her parents had promised to contribute to her household had never arrived and, as she found out later, had been given to someone else. For Hilde, there was to be no wedded bliss either. On the contrary. Her husband had turned out to be a user and a drunk who could not hold a job, wasted her money on alcohol, and expected her to keep his smelly clothes clean and have wonderful dinners ready for him whenever he deigned to show up. What she wouldn't have given for a little love and consideration! But all she was left with was grief, debts, and, after a miserable year or two, a nasty divorce.

Feeling doomed to an existence of drudgery, deprivation, and loneliness, Hilde was tempted to end it all. What eventually lifted her depression was the affection she saw in her patients' eyes. They actually appreciated her and smiled at her, and Hilde, so downtrodden most of her life, could hardly believe it. She realized that if she could cheer someone up or help him walk, her life must have meaning and must be worth preserving. She would never be rich but might find happiness by opening herself up to trust and friendship.

Hilde's long years of abuse, pain, and hard work had left their mark on her features. She looked anxious and drawn until a sudden giggle lit up her face, transforming sadness into radiance. Laughter softened her wrinkles and put sparkles in her eyes. No beauty, she, however, did her best to be presentable. Her short brown hair was always neatly trimmed and her clothes, although simple, were fresh and clean.

Longing for companionship, Hilde started going out after work, half-heartedly at first and only with colleagues, and, after she had gained in confidence, also by herself. Her favorite place was a little pub where she spent many an evening, having a good time just talking, listening to music, or playing trivia or board games. She enrolled in night classes to learn how to knit and crochet and made up her mind to pay closer attention to her neighbors, especially Sylvia who seemed very pleasant.

CHAPTER

Sylvia, at forty-five about ten years younger than Hilde, had been born under a lucky star although initially that was not the way it looked. Too young and immature to ensure her welfare, her biological parents had entrusted her to a sweet couple in their thirties who adopted her and cherished her as if she were their own flesh and blood.

They were both good-natured and comfortable to be around. They filled their home with laughter and happiness, treated Sylvia with love and respect, and gave her the freedom she needed. Sylvia, in turn, realizing how extraordinarily blessed she was, vowed to follow the admirable example her parents had set and treated her fellow human beings with the same sweetness and kindness as they had shown her.

Wherever Sylvia went, she brightened people's days, with a smile, a friendly hello, or a helping hand. She worked as a travel agent until the young man she had been engaged to for close to a year, the love of her life, suddenly weakened, gradually losing his strength and vitality. Diagnosed with leukemia, Robert's future was bleak. When Sylvia found out, there was not the least doubt in her mind that she was meant to care for him, and, without a second thought, she gave up her job to look after him as long as she was needed.

For several months she nursed him devotedly and tenderly until there was no more hope, and he died. The descendant of a well-to-do family, he had provided for her during his last days by ensuring that she would permanently receive a monthly allowance from his estate. Sylvia was devastated by his loss and touched to tears by his generosity. She never needed to work again but sitting at home with nothing constructive to do was not her idea of a meaningful life. So she went back to her job but cut her hours in half so she would have enough time to assist others in any capacity she possibly could.

Years later, while volunteering for a support group for patients suffering from depression, Sylvia met Fred, a likable man in his seventies, who was unable to deal with his wife's terminal illness and looming death. She had been bedridden for almost a decade and probably would not last much longer. When Sylvia learned the reason for his sadness, she saw an uncanny parallel to her own life and was so moved that she decided to befriend him and do whatever she could to lift his spirits, adding him to the list of people for whom she ran errands and with whom she spent time when they felt lonely.

Sylvia's appearance reflected the beauty and goodness of her heart. Nature had endowed her with a smooth and delicate face, laughing brown eyes, golden ringlets, a melodic voice, and a dainty build. She loved to wear soft pink lipstick, a little mascara, tiny earrings, and a fine gold necklace with an angel pendant. Her clothes were unique and always smart and stylish.

She was light-hearted, playful, and a breath of fresh air. Invariably people smiled when they saw her. She loved to sit in her sunny living room, looking at the beautiful angels that were hanging from her ceiling and watching her crystals glint in the light. She regularly wrote sweet notes to friends and acquaintances to remind them that she was there to support them whenever they needed her or cheer them up when their daily problems got them down. A spiritual person, she created peace and minimized strife wherever she went.

CHAPTER

H ans and Frieda were the salt of the earth, friendly, helpful, principled, and dependable. Hans, a stocky man with wisps of gray hair combed straight up with the help of a dab of brilliantine, had moved to town with his wife Frieda after his retirement from farming years ago. Hans and Frieda looked almost like twins, with Frieda, pretty plump herself, eccentrically wearing her salt-and-pepper hair in small tufts, each held together with a ribbon in subdued colors roughly matching her outfit of the day. They both had round and open faces and similar mannerisms, and looked at the world with equal optimism.

Married for close to fifty years, they still smiled at each other, their eyes shining with love, just as they had on the day they first met. Their two little grandchildren were at the center of their lives. It was their visits Hans and Frieda impatiently but happily awaited, and when they finally heard their sweet voices and the ringing of the doorbell, they ran to welcome them with big hugs and, although not particularly well-off, managed to surprise them with modest but thoughtfully chosen presents whenever they could.

Hans and Frieda loved order and cleanliness, and when Hans had first noticed that his neighbors failed to take their assigned turns of sweeping and mopping the stairs seriously, he had appointed himself voluntary custodian of the building. He still filled this role today, making his rounds every morning, thoroughly removing any dirt that he could detect while whistling like a bird. He willingly did chores for his fellow occupants and made small repairs in their homes but he did have his limits. Whereas he kindly responded to polite and reasonable requests, he disliked taking orders, which caused quite a bit of friction between him and Olga who generally did not ask for favors but rather insisted on them since she felt they were her due.

Olga's demands on her husband infuriated Frieda. Why should Hans do the lazy and spoiled woman's chores, she asked herself, grumbling that he did not get a penny from any of them, and that especially Olga could easily afford to pay a handyman to come and do her bidding. But, of course, Olga was too cheap for that and always wanted something for nothing. Whereas Frieda would have put her foot down and flatly refused to comply, Hans, anxious to preserve the peace in the building at all costs, felt it was easier to give in than start a fight with Olga. Well aware of Hans's good nature, Olga had no qualms at all about using it to her benefit, which riled Frieda to the point that, at the mere thought of Olga's manipulating her husband so wickedly, her normal gentleness gave way to the fierce determination to get even one day.

CHAPTER

These were the four people whom Olga reluctantly invited into her home although Frieda was so "honored" only because she was Hans's wife. Ordinarily they would have gotten together for coffee in the shared yard where all who lived in the building were welcome. Hilde, Sylvia, Hans and Frieda, therefore, found it quite odd that they were asked to come to Olga's flat instead on that particular afternoon. Strange, they thought, since none of them had ever entered Olga's personal space. What was she up to, they wondered, until Olga explained that the purpose of their meeting in private was to put their heads together and come up with a way to effectively deal with the blight with which Agnes and her brood were infecting the neighborhood.

What they had expected, however, was not at all what happened. As soon as they had stepped through Olga's door, she stopped them in their tracks in the narrow hallway to point out the gallery of old sepia photographs hanging along the wall. It was a display of her life she was proud of. Averse to admitting people into her flat, she had never had occasion to show it off. So this was Olga's first chance to reminisce with her neighbors, and she got carried away, telling them the stories connected to the faces staring out at them from their frames.

The first picture showed Olga's parents, her father, a tall thin man with an oversized mustache and what looked like a sooty toupee, dressed in a dark suit, stiff and conspicuously uncomfortable, and her mother, a stout matronly woman who wore her hair rigidly pulled back into a chignon. To Olga's guests, neither of them looked too likable, an impression confirmed by Olga who described them as correct in their conduct but grim and forbidding to Olga as a child although less so to her younger sister Trudi. For Trudi, Olga remembered, had always been the favorite for whom her parents had had infinite time and patience while she herself had often been banished to her room where she could be neither seen nor heard.

"There is Trudi," Olga said, moving on to the next picture which featured an apparently shy but smiling little girl with whom Olga must have competed for the limited affection her parents were capable of. There were two incidents involving Trudi that Olga mentioned to her guests since they stood out in her mind and heavily weighed on her to this day. The first one was her parents' choice to protect Trudi from the drenching rain when a sudden downpour surprised the family during an outing, totally ignoring Olga who ended up soaked to the bones. After eighty years just thinking about it still brought tears to Olga's eyes as did her recollection of the second event that had left her equally hurt and distraught. It was her parents coming to Trudi's rescue first when both girls playing in the sandbox behind their house were covered with ants and screaming for help.

Listening to Olga's account, Sylvia, Hans and Frieda, and, to a lesser extent, Hilde sympathized with Olga's pain although they all knew that Olga could neither forget nor forgive any slights or acts of injustice, even if just imagined, and that these tended to become magnified in her mind. But regardless of how Olga had turned out, they understood how she must have felt as a child, always playing second fiddle to her sister. From her perspective, there must have been two sides, with her on one and her family on the other.

As they listened to Olga, they slowly came to see her in a more human light, lending a milder dimension to her usual haughtiness and self-righteousness. Sylvia, especially, was saddened to hear that Trudi who had grown up to become a friendly and caring young woman had been struck and killed by a careless driver on her way home from work. Like she had herself, Olga, too, had lost someone close to her and must have buried her sorrow deep under her seemingly indifferent exterior.

Sylvia was right. When Trudi died, Olga initially went through the motions of mourning but could not cry. She even begrudged her sister the expense of her beautiful coffin with its frilly pink lining. Eventually, however, it hit her just how much Trudi had really meant to her and that, had she tried, they might have bridged their differences and gone through thick and thin together as real sisters do, each supporting the other.

But it was too late. All Olga could do now was attempt to repair the relationship between her and her parents. Knowing that there would never be genuine love, she kept hoping at least for some signs of recognition and warmth for her on their part, especially since she was their only surviving child, and their shared grief should have brought them closer together. Regrettably, her parents withdrew from her even further, remaining unavailable to her and keeping her at a distance. "Can you imagine how that feels," she asked her guests. "When my father died soon after, my mother went into seclusion, leaving me all alone to fend for myself."

What a sob story, was Hilde's spontaneous reaction. What happened to me was much worse, she thought, and I am not whining about it. Besides, Olga was a grown woman by then, and even if it was a bad situation, she's had six decades to get over it. Life hasn't been a bed of roses for any of us, she reflected, but then scolded herself for perhaps being too hard on Olga who, in spite of her faults, was still a human being with feelings and dreams.

Enough, Hans and Frieda were thinking as one, enough already. Like Hilde and Sylvia, initially filled with pity and compassion for the child Olga had once been, they were now wondering just how much longer she would dwell on her life. Had she forgotten the purpose of their visit, and what did any of this have to do with Agnes? They furtively glanced at their companions to find out if they felt the same way. Hilde looked back at them, rolling her eyes. But Sylvia gave nothing away. Her face was composed and pleasant, as always careful not to hurt anyone's sensibilities, not even Olga's, regardless of how she herself was feeling inside.

It had crossed Sylvia's mind that, for Olga, talking about old hurts might be a kind of therapy, allowing her to let go of them once and for all. Less perceptive and charitable than Sylvia, the others could see no justification for their still having to stand in the hallway, rooted to their spots. It seemed a huge imposition. But no one dared say a word. It would not have made any difference anyway since Olga, as usual, was determined to finish what she had set out to do.

Consideration for others had never been Olga's strong point. Oblivious of her listeners' discomfort, she resumed her story. With a scowl on her face, she pointed to the third picture which showed her estranged cousins and their offspring. "I can't stand any of them," she complained. "If they were not part of my family's history, I would not have them on my wall. I have not communicated with them for years. The only thing they want is my money." "Useless people waiting for a hand-out" was Olga's final comment on these relatives, and at the idea of their being left empty-handed in the end, a devious smile crossed her face.

Gradually Olga's continuous and persistent babble turned into a background noise that washed over her guests as their thoughts strayed to the chores they could be doing and the fun they could be having. Rather than being stuck in Olga's hallway, they could be sitting in the sun and enjoying the fragrance of jasmine in bloom.

Unfortunately for them, there were more pictures to come, beginning with number four, Olga's boss. Poor man, they were thinking, knowing that it was almost impossible to fire someone holding a civil service position like Olga's. He must have been a saint to put up with her arrogance all those years. No wonder he looked so harried and emaciated. Olga insisted that he did not appreciate her work or give her the recognition she deserved. After all, she was the only one in the office capable of doing things properly whereas her colleagues were worthless. This, knowing Olga, her listeners found hard to believe, to say the least. Most likely, they suspected, all she did was shove paperwork from one side of her desk to the other, waiting for retirement. And there was no doubt in their minds that she had made life so difficult for her coworkers with her backstabbing that they must have breathed a sigh of relief when she finally did retire.

By now, Olga was close to losing her audience altogether, their eyes glazing over with boredom. But she was not finished yet. "Pay attention," she admonished them, "and you might be amazed at my standing in the community. Do you know who that is, enjoying my company in the next picture? It's the mayor himself. Can you imagine? We talked at length at a charity event benefitting rare and injured birds, and he was more than willing to listen to my concerns."

What, of all places, was Olga doing there, Hilde, Sylvia, Hans and Frieda were asking themselves. Since when did birds mean anything to her? And then the penny dropped: She must have joined this avian preservation society for the express purpose of meeting, socializing, and being seen with the town's most prominent citizens. That the membership fee was minimal and that she had absolutely no intention to donate to their cause, Olga, of course, kept from her guests.

These, in the meantime, were fidgeting and shifting from one foot to the other. They had been offered neither seats nor the coffee and cake they had been promised. They pointedly yawned, looked at their watches, cleared their throats, and whispered to each other. "Quiet," Olga warned, "or you will miss the best picture of all, that of my fiancé."

It was much bigger than the others and the only one in full color, not just sepia. "Isn't it beautiful," Olga asked. "It's the man whom I loved and who loved me when I was young and attractive. But I had to get rid of him in the end. He was not worthy of me. He married someone inferior on the rebound and later killed himself by stepping in front of a train, still pining for me," Olga concluded and then offered to take her company to the exact location where, as shown in the newspaper article she had saved, the tragedy had occurred.

No one was curious or morbid enough to take her up on her offer. None of them cared. They were all numb with the exception of Frieda who had perked up as soon as she had set eyes on the picture. For she had recognized it. It was a photograph she had seen in one of the magazines about European royalty and celebrities that she subscribed to and, when finished with them, regularly passed along to Olga. If her memory served her correctly, it was the picture of a minor sovereign whose name and country she had forgotten. Without thinking of the consequences, she blurted out: "Isn't that the prince that was featured in the last issue?"

If looks could kill, Frieda would have been dead. Rage contorted Olga's face, and her eyes stabbed Frieda with their loathing. "How dare you question my veracity," Olga screamed, bristling with indignation. "Are you calling me a liar and a fraud?" Startled out of their drowsiness and indifference by Olga's shrill voice, Hilde, Sylvia, and Hans joined the fray on Frieda's behalf. "Do not glare at my wife," Hans warned Olga. "If you ever yell at her again or intimidate her in any way, you will have to deal with me, and I promise you it will not be pleasant."

"I agree with Frieda," added Sylvia. "It does look like the picture has been clipped from some kind of publication. But why would you do that," she asked. "Is it because you were embarrassed that you never did have a fiancé and didn't want people to think you weren't pretty or good enough for a man to notice you? So you had to invent one?" "Or maybe you did have a fiancé," Hilde threw in, "and he ran off because you treated him like you have treated all of us today, leaving us standing in your hallway, helplessly subjected to your droning on and on."

Frieda alone said nothing. She who hated to make waves and had always swallowed Olga's insults without defending herself only smiled. She had already had her revenge by casting doubt on Olga's integrity, thus compromising her scrupulously guarded image of propriety and righteousness. She had also finally paid Olga back for the many times that, under the pretense of just watering the flowers on her balcony, she, out of pure malice, had poured streams of water on Hans's and her balcony and on the neighbors walking in the garden below.

Confronted with Frieda's satisfied grin, her husband's threat, and the disturbing insinuations of the other two, Olga could not contain herself. The intensity of her fury turned her face beet-red and made her incoherent. While a stranger might have feared for Olga's sanity and well-being, her guests knew that she was a tough old bird and that there was nothing to worry about on that account. And they were right. Olga finally caught her breath and, shouting "get out, get out now," abruptly pushed them out the door.

Hilde, Sylvia, Hans and Frieda were relieved. Hilde confessed she would have exploded, had she had to listen to any more of Olga's memoirs. Sylvia, tired and upset over the falling-out, was anxious to get back to her sunny and peaceful flat. And Hans and Frieda were just in time to watch the latest episode of their favorite soap opera.

CHAPTER

How could anything go so wrong, they eventually asked themselves. They gave credit to Olga for recognizing the menace that Agnes's family posed to the safety of their neighborhood, and for that they were grateful. Initially perfectly willing to brainstorm together to come up with a solution, they were sorry that their purpose had been so completely derailed. Olga had made it vividly clear that she no longer welcomed them into her home, which most likely meant that she did not have the slightest intention to extend another offer to them to help her put an end to the petty crime encroaching upon the area. So the problem remained, and, although worried and disappointed, the neighbors agreed to give Olga time to think about it and hopefully feel comfortable enough to enlist their support again in the future.

For the moment, however, they were much more curious about Olga's love life. Had her fiancé ever existed? They were intrigued. Judging by Olga's propensity of being consumed with herself and invariably insisting on getting her way, they could hardly imagine her having a pleasant relationship with a man or captivating one with her charm in the first place. It was unthinkable.

Sylvia alone could see it. "Let's give her the benefit of the doubt," she suggested. "People do change, especially over decades, and it is conceivable there might have been such a person. Maybe Olga did not have a picture of him or perhaps lost it and therefore used someone else's instead. It's possible. Whether or not Olga had indeed had a fiancé is a question only she herself can answer." But no one dared to ask.

As for Olga, she was livid that her guests had had the gall to question her engagement. How could this happen to her? Left to stew in her living room, she convinced herself that they had fully deserved to be thrown out. For they had not only dealt a serious blow to her pride but also thoughtlessly choked off her project of keeping the neighborhood safe. Incredulous that, for once, things were not going her way and utterly frustrated, she cursed the very people she had previously favored with her invitation. "Ingrates," she screamed, startling Fluffy out of his doze. Coddled his entire life, he was not used to such outbursts. He raised his head, yelped in protest, and went back to sleep, obviously disinterested in commiserating with Olga, which incensed her even more and prompted her to give free reign to her exasperation.

It was Frieda who became her primary target. "Who is this woman to doubt me? What appalling manners! Did anyone ever tell her to respect her elders and superiors? If they did, Frieda didn't listen. She's a nobody and has never accomplished anything in her entire life," Olga raved and ranted, ignoring conveniently that Frieda and Hans had worked hard and tirelessly to raise three children to become decent citizens who now had families of their own. None of them had ever been on welfare or in trouble with the law, quite an achievement in today's world. To Olga that meant nothing at all. For her it was simple: Common people did not belong in her circle, and diminishing herself to include Frieda and Hans had been a mistake she would not repeat.

To physically express her contempt, she ran to the kitchen with a vengeance, grabbed a large pail, filled it with water, and poured it down on Hans and Frieda's balcony, turning over some of their flower pots and destroying the seedlings Frieda had carefully tended.

A malicious smirk on her face, she then went back inside to contemplate Hilde's and Sylvia's punishment for siding with Hans and Frieda. What had she expected, she asked herself. Both Sylvia and Hilde, too, were obviously below her in stature, just not as far down as Hans and Frieda. As for Hilde, Olga was planning to smear her reputation by spreading subtle rumors about her frequenting a disreputable bar and carrying on with married men. And on top of that, she would threaten her with a change in her will, crushing her hopes of ever inheriting her flat if she did not toe the line.

Sylvia would not fare any better. Intensely jealous of her beauty, Olga had long been waiting for a chance to discredit her. Sylvia looked like an angel, and everyone seemed to enjoy being around her. Olga begrudged her particularly the attraction she held for men, just as she begrudged all married women their husbands. What irked Olga equally was the fact that Sylvia apparently never put on a single ounce of fat whereas Olga herself found it extremely difficult to keep her weight down. Sylvia's defying Olga over the picture was the last straw in the string of grievances Olga harbored against her.

The cleverness of her intended revenge caused Olga a great deal of amusement: She would spread the word that Sylvia's skinniness was due to giving herself enemas on a daily basis, and that her friendship with Fred was suspect and immoral.

Olga could not wait to put her plan into action. She set out to make the rounds of all the shops she normally frequented to spew her poison. On the way, the first person she saw was a beggar bundled up on the pavement, with his tin cup in front of him and his German shepherd on a blanket beside him. "Hey, you," Olga accosted him, "don't you know that this is no way to treat animals? It's a disgrace! Do you have a permit for the dog, and are you authorized to be here?" The tin she deliberately overlooked as she had no sympathy at all for the poor and would never spend a penny of her money to help them. The beggar pretended not to hear her as he knew from past encounters with Olga that it was useless to fight a war of words with her, a war he could not win.

Having dealt with the beggar, Olga felt drained and realized she had missed out on her afternoon coffee and cake. So she entered a café to sit down and enjoy an espresso and a huge piece of apfelstru-del with whipped cream before continuing on her rounds. Sophie, the waitress, had seen her coming. Oh no, she thought, not that nasty woman again. I don't need any more aggravation today and could use a nice tip. But Frau Lindermann doesn't give tips. She is the customer from hell. No matter how hard I try, I cannot please her. She whines about everything: her coffee is too strong or too weak, and her cake too firm or too soggy. Nothing is ever right, and I am tired of it! If she showed up more often, I would quit!

To Sophie's surprise, Olga was considerably less combative that day. She was too much in a hurry to pursue her agenda to pay atten-tion to either the appearance or the taste of her order. Without whin-ing about anything—kuchen, beverage, or service—she soon got up and paid her bill, neglecting, as usual, to round it up, which meant that, again, there was no tip. But, at least, there had been no harsh words either, and Sophie was relieved.

Olga's next stop was the butcher shop where she encountered a long line of people already waiting to be served. To get ahead of them, she, with typical nerve, elbowed her way through to the front. Regardless of how loudly the other customers grumbled or how hard they pushed, jostled, or shoved her, past experience had taught them that Olga would never budge. Once at the counter, she would take her own sweet time, inspecting the meats and sausages and com-menting on their quality. She would sample and probe here and there until she would finally make up her mind what to buy and—the last straw for everyone present—insist on a juicy lagniappe for Fluffy, and that is exactly what she did.

Even after putting her purchases in her bag, Olga lingered, chal-lenging the other shoppers who by now had murder on their minds. They were the perfect audience, she realized, and she could hold them captive as long as she pleased. After all, she had something to say, and say it she would. So, without any scruples on her part, she stared them down and launched into a vicious attack on Hilde's and Sylvia's character and morals.

Olga had not counted on Agnes, however, whom she had not noticed in the queue. Agnes, having nothing to gain by being nice to Olga, had no compunctions about crossing swords with her at all. "Olga," she lashed out, "you self-righteous old bag! Quit sticking your nose in where you are not wanted! If you believe you are the perfect saint who has never done anything wrong, you are delusional. I have news for you: You are just as damnable as anybody else. So stop trumpeting the misdeeds of others you know nothing about and instead entertain us with your own!"

A gratified titter rippled through the shop. Olga, as if stung by a tarantula, lunged forward to shake Agnes. "You are a fine one to talk," she sputtered, "you with your delinquent brood and your husband walking out on you! You don't know whom you are dealing with! First of all, do not ever call me "Olga" again! To you, I am "Frau Lindermann," remember that! No one calls me by my first name! But no one! I am the only one who bestows this honor, and I do so exclusively on those who have earned that right over a lifetime! You are definitely not one of them and never will be. Secondly, don't you ever dare even suggest that I have shortcomings! I am so much better than any of you," and having said that, she stormed out of the store with her head held up high.

Olga's next destination was the vegetable and fruit kiosk. To get there, she had to cross the street. No one could ever force her to use the pedestrian crossing or yield to any vehicle. Not Olga. She felt that to be kept waiting was below her dignity. So, propelled by her anger and frustration, she walked straight into the traffic to loud protests, screeching tires, and honking horns, which did not bother her in the least. After all, she was entitled.

The vendor heard the commotion, saw Olga approaching, and was filled with dread at the idea of having to deal with her as she had the disgusting habit of grabbing everything, poking, pinching, and prodding, picking up an apple here and a head of cauliflower there before eventually making a decision. He was far from pleased when she attempted to drag Sylvia and Hilde through the mud and made it clear he did not want to listen to her gossip. "Madam," he said, "I know neither one of these individuals personally and would not attempt to make a judgment." Thus censured, Olga turned on her heel with a contemptuous flounce and took off in a huff.

Enough for today, she decided. It was getting late and Fluffy had to be fed. So she returned home, put away her purchases, poured out the coffee long cold under its cozy, and rewrapped the stale ready-made cake she had meant to serve her guests for use at another time. She then took care of Fluffy who occupied her only armchair and sank down into the sofa cushions to relax with a tabloid.

C H A P T E R

But she could not concentrate. Her eyes wandered from page to page without really seeing anything. Her failed errand had left her down and deflated. Her eyes skimmed over her living room crowded with her parents' heavy black furniture and the deep-olive velvet drapes that kept out much of the sunlight during the day. They briefly rested on her multitude of crocheted doilies, countless knick-knacks, and the odd Hummel figurine, and then shifted to the grayish walls that could have greatly benefitted from a fresh coat of paint.

What she didn't see, or didn't want to see, was the dust she occasionally swept from one surface to another with her acid-green feather duster or the dirt on the brownish linoleum floor which, most likely, had not been mopped in years. The windows, too, were grimy, especially on the bottom where Fluffy had smeared them with his slobber.

It was a singularly dreary space, decorated only with newspaper clippings in cheap frames and a few drab traditional landscapes and still lifes. There was no real color, and neither was there a single innovative or cheerful piece of art since something as bold as a red elephant or a blue dog would have offended Olga's sensibilities.

Even if there had been an exciting picture, it would not have registered with Olga that night. Her lids were getting heavy, and she soon fell sound asleep. It was pitch-dark outside although the light of the moon outlined a black cat jumping from a tree onto the railing of Olga's balcony and from there into her living room. It had bright-red fiery eyes and sharp fangs, and emitted a sickening stench. When it reached Olga, it confronted her with bloodcurdling howls. Olga attempted to get away but could not move. She shrank into herself, and, as the beast was getting bigger and bigger and more and more menacing, she felt completely exposed and helpless. She was trembling, her heart was pounding, and, utterly terrified, she began to sob.

But the cat knew no mercy. It attacked Fluffy, devoured a bird on Olga's balcony, dug up the soil in her flowerpots, and deposited its waste. Then it returned to wherever it had come from, and Olga woke up. Tears were running down her cheeks as she realized that it had all been a ghastly dream. Trying to compose herself, she got up from the couch and stumbled into bed.

The next morning, she was afraid to open her eyes, afraid of what she might see. She wished she could be certain that the cat had been nothing but a creation of her nightmare. It had been so real and incredibly scary. Olga would never admit it but, even now, she was profoundly shaken. She checked her flowerpots to reassure herself that they had not been touched, and when she found them intact, sat down by Fluffy, comforted by his presence.

"I don't feel well at all this morning," she said to him, "and I am so glad you are here. I wish you could talk to me and tell me why and how it was possible for such a horrifying dream to creep into my mind. I wonder what it could mean. Some people might say that it was my conscience troubling me. But I have never understood that theory and do not believe it. I don't feel guilty about anything but, just in case there is something to this ridiculous notion, what in the world could have created such torment in my head? Was it because I might have slightly antagonized my neighbors, or do you think it was the little white lie I told about Albert?"

"What happened with the neighbors, you know already, Fluffy. You were here. But Albert is another story. Frieda was right: The picture showed some unknown prince, not Albert. And Albert was not my fiancé either but the boy next-door whom I liked so much that I was always hoping he would be my husband one day."

"After losing track of him for three or four years, I suddenly spotted him on the street. He was just as handsome as ever, and I couldn't let him get away again. But Albert was not happy to see me. He was married, he said, and asked me to leave him alone. And yet, I was so sure he had feelings for me and would eventually get a divorce that I confronted him on two other occasions, only to be rejected again. But I didn't give up."

"I was determined to try one last time. That's when he lost his temper. 'Leave me alone,' he screamed. 'I have told you and told you that I am married, and even when I was still single, I couldn't stand you! Always hanging around! What do you want with me? Just because we were neighbors when we were children, and our parents might have had some sort of misguided understanding as to our future, what gives you the idea you have a claim on me?'"

"Oh, Fluffy, it looked so hopeless but I just couldn't let it go. Desperate to save whatever ties there might have been between us, I held on to him but he managed to tear himself away. When I begged him to stay, he looked at me with contempt in his eyes, turned around, and fled. You can't imagine, Fluffy, how humiliated I felt. It was my entire life and all my hopes he had just crushed, dismissing me as if I were a venomous insect. How dare he do that to me, I asked myself, and more determined than ever to make him notice and love me, I ran after him as fast as I could."

"When I was finally getting closer, Albert, perhaps to throw me off, unexpectedly veered to the right to cross the train tracks. I suppose he was so focused on getting rid of me that he didn't look up to see the crossing gates come down. And neither did he listen to the warning signal of the approaching train. I will never forget the jarring sound of the impact. It killed him instantly."

"Albert's death was initially investigated as a matter of routine as were all accidents involving public transport. And the findings clearly pointed to Albert as the responsible party until a witness came forward to testify that, shortly before he was killed, he was being chased by a woman whom she identified as me, Olga."

"This I readily admitted. 'I thought the young man looked like he was bent on committing suicide so I pursued him to save his life,' I told them. 'I could have stopped him if I hadn't been so slow. It's all my fault,' I added, putting on such a display of tears and sorrow that the investigators were convinced that the deceased had been a stranger to me, and that I had nothing to do with his death."

Olga had been so caught up in her memories that she had almost forgotten Fluffy's presence and her original intention of confessing her peccadillos so she would no longer be plagued by nightmares. But she had gone on too long, and poor Fluffy was sound asleep. Reluctant to wake him up to tell him the rest of the story, Olga decided to continue, hoping that, whether Fluffy heard it or not, for her it would mean the end of bad dreams.

"The morning after the tragedy," she recalled, "the local paper published a picture of the dreadful accident which thankfully did not include me, and the text did not refer to me by name but simply called me a bystander. So no one was aware of any potential link between me and the deceased. And soon Albert's death faded into oblivion."

"As the years went by, however, I became more and more anxious about being mocked as the proverbial old maid and started toying with the idea of somehow reviving and using Albert's memory to keep the busybodies at bay. And one day, I hit upon a version of my unfortunate experience with Albert that would admirably serve my purpose. It was total fiction, of course, but would satisfy people's curiosity and considerably improve my image at the same time. No longer the spinster that nobody wanted, I transformed myself into the desirable woman Albert could not live without and, consequently, decided to end it all."

"This is more or less the account I gave Hilde, Frieda, Sylvia, and Hans when they were here yesterday. As you know, Fluffy, it's false, but don't you think it's clever? I even managed to put my own spin on Albert's marriage! Aren't you proud of me? I am still congratulating myself for thinking of it. And here is my proof in black and white: the clipping from the paper about the accident that I have held onto all these years. So, Fluffy, I am fully vindicated and deserve to be admired for having been faithful to my dead fiancé all my life."

"Now that I have told you the whole story, Fluffy, I should be entirely free of nightmares. No more twinges of conscience, as they say. To be honest, I really don't know what that means. I only did what I had to do. So why should it bother me? And, Fluffy, look at my hand! See that ring? It was my mother's, but doesn't it look like a promise ring to you? You must admit, I am shrewd, ingenious, and still pretty fetching for my age."

C H A P T E R

Olga was relieved, thinking that, by coming clean about her imaginary engagement to Albert, she had dispelled the likelihood of bad dreams assailing her in the future. But the harrowing memory of the previous night lingered nevertheless. To distract herself, Olga resolved to go for a stroll in the park. For once, she did not take Fluffy as she had no desire to make small talk with the other dog owners she might encounter. She headed for the lake where a family of ducks were moving about among the reeds. To observe them more closely, Olga followed the winding path that gently descended toward the water's edge. It was dappled with sunlight and lined with fragrant purplish-blue and white lilacs alive with the sweet chirps of tiny birds in their branches. Two squirrels were playing, chasing each other from tree to tree, and iridescent dragonflies were flitting through the crisp and sparkling air.

As Olga approached the huge willows and clumps of bulrushes circling the lake, church bells began to ring in the distance. How beautiful they sound, Olga reflected and admired the glorious nature around her. It was a wonderful place of peace that slowly dissipated her anxiety and filled her with calm.

As soon as the ducks became aware of Olga's presence, they swam toward her, expecting to be fed. To her regret, she was empty-handed. In her hurry to get out of the house and forget all about her nightmare, bringing treats for them had completely slipped Olga's mind. I hope they don't take offense, Olga was thinking. She wanted them to stay a while and keep her company, and they did. Being with them and watching them in this lovely setting warmed her heart, and, with a smile on her face, she then quietly retraced her steps so as not to disturb the birds welcoming the day with their songs.

Following the trail, she came to an old fountain, with a golden angel on top of the center column. It reminded her of the angels in Sylvia's living room, and suddenly Olga's animosity toward her neighbor faded, and she wished they could be on speaking terms once again. Her attitude toward Hilde, too, softened somewhat. Hilde, after all, had been kind enough to create the countless outfits for Fluffy that kept him warm and comfortable. Both Sylvia and Hilde were people Olga could relate to, and she made up her mind—not to stoop to an apology—but at least to exchange a few words with them the next time they met.

It was such a gorgeous morning that Olga could not resist sitting down on the circular stone bench surrounding the fountain. She listened to the water tumbling from the angel's hands and marveled at the stunning flower beds the city had planted at her feet. There were thousands of blossoms in different shapes, sizes, and colors, all buzzing with bees. Olga was entranced. She had come here to seek solace, and she had found it.

In her mellow mood, she thought of Zora whose garden she glimpsed at a distance. Although Olga had always heard how wonderful and amazing it was, she had never seen it for herself. Curious to find out what the excitement was all about, she took the path leading to Zora's fence, and what appeared in front of her eyes was a paradise of flowers, even prettier than she could ever have imagined. She was spellbound. In her rapture, she failed to notice Zora who was sitting motionless on her porch and, to her utter amazement, detected an actual smile on Olga's face.

For quite a while, Olga just stood there, mesmerized and oblivious to everything but the beauty before her. She still had not become aware of Zora who had gotten up and was now standing at the railing, calling out to Olga and inviting her to join her on the porch. Olga was startled, torn out of her reverie. She initially hesitated to enter Zora's property because she had always thought of Zora as a member of the lower classes with whom she ordinarily would not associate. But she did not hesitate for long. I may have misjudged Zora, she grudgingly admitted to herself, conceding that someone who creates such beauty cannot be all bad.

After shaking hands, the two sat together comfortably, Olga resting her legs and enjoying a slice of homemade cake and a cup of coffee. Their conversation, at first awkward and halting in view of the past, became more animated, however, when they discovered that, in addition to their love of flowers, newly found in Olga's case, they also shared a love for their pets. And when Max came flying and alighted on his spot on the railing, they laughed together until, running out of things to say to each other, they parted in apparent harmony.

But both had second thoughts, and doubt crept into their minds. Zora was wary. She did not trust the sudden change in Olga. Isn't it too late for Olga at her age to turn over a new leaf, she asked herself. Is she even capable of being sincere? Zora was not convinced. She was uneasy, and so was Olga. What possessed me to set foot in Zora's house, she wondered. I must have been carried away by the sight of the beautiful flowers. And now I owe her an invitation! If I don't reciprocate, what will people think of me? It would simply not be proper. But if I ask her to come to my home, what would my neighbors say? After weighing the pros and cons, she decided that, to save face, it might be best for her to invite Zora to lunch at a little restaurant where no one knew her—just not any time soon.

Zora was still mulling over the situation when a friendly hello announced Adi who came jumping over the fence. "Our lofty neighbor, what was she doing here," he wanted to know. "I am not sure," Zora answered truthfully because she was still puzzled by Olga's acceptance of her invitation which she probably should not have extended in the first place. "It's all so difficult. We did have a nice conversation but was it genuine? I honestly don't know. Do I regret it? Only time will tell."

Adi really cared about Zora. He knew what a good person she was and did not ever want her feelings to get hurt. Practical by nature and never too shy to express his opinion, he came right out and warned his friend: "That woman is nosy," he said. "Just be careful! Who knows what rumors she will be spreading about you next."

Olga meanwhile pondered her own unexpected interest in flowers. It surprised her since she had always felt self-sufficient and complete and had never seen the need to educate herself any further—until now. She was so intrigued by Zora's plants that she wanted to learn all about them. And Zora would have been the perfect teacher if Olga's pride had allowed her to ask for her help. "I couldn't bear seeing the pity in Zora's eyes when she realizes that I know nothing about gardening at all," Olga said to herself. "It would be too humiliating." And in the end she decided she would go elsewhere to find out more about the flowers that so delighted her.

CHAPTER

The next morning Olga set out to look at another garden, one she had missed the day before. It was Agnes's. When she peeked over the fence, she was sorely disappointed. Agnes's garden was strictly utilitarian, bleak, and almost bare of flowers. Weeds competed for light and ground with neglected vegetables, and the shrubs were still dripping from last night's rain. Everything looked dark and dead whereas Zora's garden was a riot of color, teeming with life.

In a corner Olga spotted a pile of broken furniture and wondered what it was doing there. No doubt Agnes's home was heated with oil so she definitely would not be able to use it to keep warm in the winter. The wood had to serve another purpose, and, looking more closely, she soon understood that it was there to cover up hundreds of empty wine bottles. "I always knew that family was unhinged, and now it looks like they are drunks as well," Olga snorted. What she did not know and could not have imagined was how the furniture had been broken in the first place.

"You call this a garden," Olga loudly reflected. "It's a disaster! I can do so much better myself, and I will," she vowed. "I will show you, Agnes! You just wait!" At that moment, she heard a loud crash and an ear-piercing scream coming from upstairs and quickly hid behind the fence. More than ever convinced of nefarious goings on in that house and now quite alarmed, she ducked and hurriedly tip-toed away, hoping that no one had noticed her presence.

At least her morning was not entirely wasted. Although having learned nothing about flowers, she had instead gained ammunition against Agnes which might turn out to be useful one day. At the thought, a sneer twisted her features. "But unfortunately that won't help me now," she reminded herself. "I still don't know any more about plants than I did this morning. How nice it would be if I could participate in the flower show in the spring, meet all the dignitaries, and perhaps even get my picture in the paper."

"But I am getting ahead of myself," she realized. What she needed were some books on gardening but all she had on her shelf were a few dog-eared primers from her childhood which unfortunately were not relevant. "What if I try the library," she wondered. "It may just have the answers I'm looking for." For Olga who had never once been in any library in her eighty plus years, it would be an entirely new experience.

Although not far, the local library was not within Olga's usual walking distance. But she was on a mission and, after grabbing a quick lunch, opted to take the bus. It was not her favorite means of transportation but it was cheap. What she mostly disliked about it was being exposed to what she called the other passengers' drivel, a potential predicament which she avoided by turning her nose up in the air and her face away from anyone who might attempt to engage her in conversation.

Having conquered the difficulty of the ride, Olga entered the library, expecting to be welcomed with open arms. Alas, that was not the case. Patrons were being helped on a first come first served basis, and Olga was last in line. When she tried to push the earlier arrivals aside, she was promptly instructed that jumping the queue was not acceptable. She had to wait her turn just like everyone else.

By the time a friendly employee finally offered to help, Olga was extremely annoyed. She briefly explained her interest and ungraciously insisted on being at once shown the best books on plants and their care available. When told that some of them had been reserved, Olga responded with a sneer and, after finally making up her mind to check out two large volumes, found herself in another line.

"What nerve," Olga protested. "Do they think I have all day?" She was outraged, especially since neither her advanced age nor her heavy load mattered enough to the staff to grant her priority, a bitter pill for Olga to swallow. She finally grabbed her books and, without a word of thanks, walked out and slammed the door. "Imbeciles," she repeatedly muttered under her breath on the way to the bus stop.

There Olga intended to drop the books on the bench and sit down while waiting for her bus. Unfortunately every single seat was taken, all of them by teen-agers who were talking and joking without paying the least attention to her, enraging Olga beyond endurance. "You," she shouted at them, "don't you respect your elders? Where are your manners? Don't you know that you are supposed to give up your seats to seniors who need them?" "So what," was the flippant reply.

If there was one thing Olga could not tolerate, it was being snubbed, especially by these toerags. Absolutely livid, she screamed: "You useless bunch, get up this instant," and that's when she recognized two of the offenders, Monika and Fabian, Agnes's younger children. They were laughing, chewing gum, and blowing bubbles toward Olga who became so infuriated by their appalling conduct that she threw the heavy library books in their direction. To her profound regret, she missed, and the books ended up on the ground, which brought insolent smirks to the faces around her. By then, Olga was so angry she could have killed them. Since none of them lifted a finger to pick up her books, Olga had to get down on her knees in front of the siblings and their sorry friends and collect them herself, which, to her, seemed to be the worst indignity she had ever suffered.

Whether unwilling to ride the bus with these hoodlums or, after her ordeal, incapable of bothering with its inconveniences, Olga allowed herself the luxury of taking a cab. She sat back in her comfortable seat, imagined confronting Agnes with the flagrant behavior of her children, and then dozed until the taxi driver gently nudged her awake at her door.

It was late and Olga was exhausted. She ate a bite, fed Fluffy, and fell into bed. But it was not to be a peaceful night. Another bad dream disrupted her sleep: Two hideous apparitions slowly emerged out of the dark and assailed her with their sharp teeth, leaving her cheeks scratched and bloody. They then licked them with their tongues, healing her skin with their saliva. As they gradually faded into a cloud and subsequently reappeared as shadowy gray stems and leaves, eventually brightening into the most beautiful orange and yellow flowers, Olga's fears subsided, and she saw her dream as a sign that she would overcome all obstacles, and all would be well in the end. She calmly got up, had breakfast, and took Fluffy for his usual morning walk in the park. It was a sunny day, and Olga, fully recovered from her nocturnal fright, was looking forward to taking a peek at her library books.

CHAPTER

The only flowers Olga had ever grown were yellow, orange, and red nasturtiums. She enjoyed watching them stretch and expand until they hung down from their boxes on the balcony, lending vivid color to the wrought-iron railings. She, of course, also knew and could identify roses, daisies, thistles, stinging nettles, irises, and the like, the most common plants she saw almost every day. But there was an entirely new world on the pages of the borrowed volumes, an endless variety of plants unknown to her, their history, origins, habitats, names, uses and care, by far too much for Olga to absorb without long hours of further study.

She was overwhelmed and beginning to doubt herself. "Am I ready for this," she wondered. "I'm in comfortable circumstances and could just sit back and relax. Why burden myself with all this learning? I've never had to make such an effort before. But then maybe my life has been somewhat humdrum and needs a little spice," she pondered, "and what better way to provide it than getting recognition for developing a unique flower of extraordinary beauty?"

Olga's vision of eventually winning first prize for her horticultural achievements was too tempting for her to ignore. Meeting the notables judging the competition and being honored by them was an idea she found irresistible. Olga's ambition took over, and her mind was made up. She would face, and successfully deal with, the impending drudgery. It would be worth it.

It was a lofty goal from which she, however, was temporarily sidetracked by a procession of ants coming from the window and invading her kitchen. Because of Fluffy, she refused to spray them with poison. Then she remembered a section in one of the books, dealing with harmless pesticides that could easily be made from plants at home. So for now, that became her priority. The ants would have to go. Determined, she set out to pore over the various formulae provided. Some were realistic, others were not, and she had the feeling that a few were myths or based on folklore alone and would not really work for her. It occurred to her that using plants freely accessible to her would speed up the demise of the ants. So she concentrated on those.

The first plant on the list which she recognized was mint. No need to buy this one, she rejoiced. I know just where it is. So she crossed the park, sneaked up to Zora's fence, and helped herself. But she did not remain unnoticed. Zora who happened to look out through her lace curtains observed Olga coming out from behind the gate, looking furtively all around her, and pulling out a number of plants. Zora was disappointed and deeply hurt. "If she had just asked, I would have gladly given them to her," she thought, "but what she is doing is stealing. It's so underhanded, and Adi is right: It pays to be cautious."

Olga had no qualms. The plants were there, and she needed them. It was that simple. Besides, Zora had so many of them that she wouldn't miss the few she had pilfered. It's not as if I had broken the law or harmed Zora in any way, Olga rationalized. To her, being unethical was a mere trifle compared to the real risk of being found out, which would have dealt an unspeakable blow to her pride. But Olga had been careful, and, confident that she had gotten away with her little escapade, she hurried home, her satisfaction reflected in her face.

Unfortunately the mint did not work as the book had predicted and Olga had hoped that it would. She lined up the leaves along the window sills as well as the kitchen counter and yet, instead of being deterred, the ants kept marching forward. She poked at them to get them to turn around and tried to guide them back to the little crack through which she had seen them enter. But they would not be stopped. They simply maneuvered around the obstacles Olga had put in their way and carried on.

"So much for this useless piece of advice," Olga sighed. "I bet the smell of the mint just wasn't pungent enough. I might have to boil the leaves and cook up a really strong decoction that will make the ants cringe and chase them away." And that's what she did. Impatient for it to work, she poured the boiling liquid on top of the ants. But, of course, it was the frightful heat that killed them—not the mint, and as soon as the puddle had cooled off somewhat, they were back. As Olga was watching, more and more were coming, attracted, rather than driven away, by the minty fragrance. It apparently animated them, and Olga was dumbfounded.

"I wonder who is writing these books," Olga grumbled. "So far they have been worthless. Let's see what they can do about the wasps that keep sitting on my plum cake." The plants recommended for getting rid of wasps were wormwood, citronella, mint, and eucalyptus. Mint Olga immediately rejected. What a waste of time. It didn't kill ants, and it won't kill wasps. She had never heard of citronella but did know the dry green-dyed stalks of eucalyptus that had turned grayish with dust after years in her vase. When she first bought them ages ago, they gave off a repulsive odor, no doubt from the chemical treatment they had undergone. Whatever original scent there had been, there was none now, which made them useless for her purpose. Her strong eucalyptus cough drops might not work any better as they contained so much sugar the wasps would probably love them. And traveling to Australia to break off fresh branches of eucalyptus was not in Olga's plans.

So that left wormwood, a name she had never come across. According to the text, it was used not only to deter wasps but also as an ingredient in absinthe and vermouth. Olga looked at the pictures and recognized it as a plant that grew in Agnes's garden. "How fitting," she exclaimed, "they all drink, and I bet they make their own liqueur! Typical! Of course, Agnes would grow it! I wonder what it tastes like." So Olga ran to Agnes's, reached over the fence, and swiped a few shoots of wormwood. This time, it was very quiet although Olga had the uncomfortable feeling they might all be standing at the window, observing her, the thought of which made her shudder. But there was no one, and Olga got away without being challenged.

As there were no instructions, Olga did not know what to do with the wormwood. So she first tried to subdue the wasps by waving the leaves at them and then dousing them with drops of an extract she had prepared herself. But it was hopeless. The wasps would not budge. "Why don't I use a little absinthe or vermouth to get rid of them," she asked herself. At the store, she was told that absinthe could not be legally sold as it had been declared detrimental to people's health. But bottles of vermouth were on the shelf. So she bought one and poured some of its contents on the wasps. They relished it, and instead of flying away, they attracted more and more of their kind. Tipsy, they staggered around on the plums.

"Another fiasco," Olga fretted. "My cake is ruined, and these infernal creatures have taken over. Shame on the authors and their so-called pesticides and insecticides! They don't know what they are talking about. But," she conceded, "in the process I learned something about Agnes and her brats that I would not have found out otherwise. Besides, unlike ordinary potions, absinthe and vermouth sound quite exotic, and the vermouth wasn't cheap by any means. Maybe I should taste it. At least I wouldn't have wasted my money," Olga reflected, poured some into an egg cup, took a little sip, and then swallowed the rest. "Not bad," she said, "I should have tried this a long time ago." Then she filled another egg cup, and another… until she dozed off with a smile on her face.

For once she slept soundly without being bothered by nightmares and woke up only when Fluffy jumped up and licked her face and hands in an attempt to rouse her. "Maybe that's what I need once in a while, a little nightcap," she mused. "Then I wouldn't have to worry about not getting enough rest or bad dreams any more. It certainly did work like a charm last night." And, indeed, Olga was uncharacteristically good-humored and no longer blamed the library staff or their books for her failed experiments. "That's water under the bridge," Olga consoled herself. "I will do better next time." Fluffy got a special treat for his patience, and both set off on their daily rounds through the park.

CHAPTER

Approaching the fountain, they encountered a young lady Olga did not recognize. Short and a little chubby, she had olive skin, shiny dark hair pulled straight back, and the sweetest expression on her face. She was wearing a long colorful skirt composed of horizontal bands of dark blue, forest green and cerise fabric and an indigo top. Olga was intrigued. "I know everyone who lives around the park," she thought, "but I am sure I have never seen this lady before. Who could she be? She really seems pleasant, and I wouldn't mind making her acquaintance." So Olga uttered a brief greeting to which the stranger responded with a friendly nod, and Olga forgot all about her plants.

Finding out the lady's identity became a priority. Because of her tan skin, Olga assumed she might be a member of one of the Turkish worker families that were brought into the country after the war to take the place of the men who had been killed. Although many had returned to their homeland, there were still quite a few of them in Bavaria, either working in textile factories like their parents or already fully integrated into German society.

Normally Olga looked down on the Turkish population but there was something about this lady that intrigued her. To discover who she was, she followed her from afar to the northwest end of the park and through a few alleyways, until she saw her crossing a courtyard and entering an outbuilding on the grounds of the Church of Our Dear Lady. "What could she be doing there," Olga wondered and then said to Fluffy: "She doesn't look like a nun to me. Let's stick around a bit and see what happens." But Fluffy did not feel like waiting forever. He got impatient and started pulling on his leash.

At that moment, the back door opened, revealing a priest whom Olga knew only by sight. She hesitated to address him since she had not set foot in a church for over seventy years, considered any religious service a waste of time, and was not even Catholic. But she could not help herself. "Sir, can you tell me whether this building contains offices or living quarters," she inquired. "I am not at liberty to say," was the priest's reply, "but if you need assistance, please go to the reception area in the old tower just around the corner."

This Olga had not foreseen. Since she did not want to appear nosy, she dropped her quest for the time being. But she was miffed, especially in view of all the other stumbling blocks she had recently come across. "What is going on," she wondered. "My neighbors and I are at odds, insects are taking over my home, and my efforts are consistently frustrated. Life used to be so easy, and I have always gotten what I wanted. But now I have lost my touch, and it looks like I have run out of luck. Come along, Fluffy," she continued, lightening up a bit, "let's go home and have a nice peaceful evening together."

On the way back to her flat, Olga heard brisk footsteps behind her that signaled the approach of the young lady who had previously piqued her curiosity. She quickly caught up with Olga, passed her, briefly turned her head and smiled, then increased her pace, and finally disappeared at the end of the path leading to Agnes's house. "Why would she be interested in Agnes," Olga pondered. "I would have liked to meet her first, but it looks like Agnes has beaten me to it. The mystery around Agnes is certainly deepening although it's too late, and I am too tired, to solve it tonight. It's time to go," she reminded Fluffy, picked him up, and headed for home.

Meanwhile, Hans and Frieda had made every effort to stay out of Olga's way. Whenever they heard her coming, they scrambled to get out of sight. As a favor to everyone, Hans continued to sweep and mop the stairwell as usual, even to Olga's door, but Frieda was not so forgiving. She no longer shared her magazines with Olga who was always itching to get her hands on them and had taken them completely for granted. "I am hoping to teach her a lesson," Frieda told Hans, "and if I succeed, she may learn to be grateful and eventually even apologize." But both were realistic enough not to hold their breath until that happened.

Sylvia and Hilde's feud with Olga had brought them closer together. They were both lonely and frequently chatted about their everyday lives, their thoughts, their work, and their friends. For now, they decided to leave Olga to her own devices although Hilde was in two minds. If she had not been so worried that Olga might have changed her will, no longer leaving her the flat, she would have been relieved because Olga's endless demands on her had become a real burden.

Whereas Hilde was torn between her hopes for a better future and the prospect of finally being free of Olga's impositions, Sylvia was sad about the falling-out. "Olga is not my favorite person," she was thinking. "She has been difficult and misguided. But she is a human being with feelings that have been hurt, deservedly or not. No wonder she has been bristling more than usual. And she's all alone. If I can help restore an atmosphere of good will between Olga and the rest of us, I will." And Sylvia sat down and appealed to her angels and the universe to bring peace.

Olga, too, missed her neighbors, in fact more so than she could have imagined or admitted. She kept trying to think of a dignified way to smooth things over without losing face although initially none crossed her mind. If she called them, they might hang up on her, leaving her even more humiliated. She could write conciliatory notes but feared she might not strike the right tone, or whatever she put down in black and white might be passed around, ridiculed, or misinterpreted. She eventually settled on leaving flowers for them, to her the only safe overture she could make.

She got hold of Fluffy, put him on his leash, and hastened toward the beautiful public flower bed by the fountain. Making sure she was unobserved, she quickly cut three sky-blue delphiniums and three yellow roses, one of each for Hilde, Sylvia, and herself. She hid them in her shopping bag and, once back in her building, taped her peace offerings on Hilde's and Sylvia's doors and put hers in a vase. "Giving flowers was a clever idea," she complimented herself, "because it's flowers I want to talk to them about."

Hilde and Sylvia were in the middle of having a bite to eat at Hilde's when they heard a noise at the door. Curious because the doorbell had not rung, Hilde looked through the peephole and saw Olga's face and arms. "Sylvia," she told her friend, "you won't believe this but it's her highness, Olga, and obviously she's not come to visit. I bet she's left a nasty note." They waited until they heard Olga's door closing, then tiptoed outside to find out what she had been doing, discovered the flowers, and had a good laugh.

Olga who had the stealthy habit of loudly shutting her door just for show and then opening it back quietly to allow her to eavesdrop on others, overheard their reaction to her "gracious" gesture and sensed their relief. She closed her door, this time for real, and came running down the stairs and along the hallway. "How do you like your flowers, Hilde," she wanted to know. "I saw them at the store this morning and immediately thought of you and Sylvia. Sylvia, yours are at your door. Aren't they beautiful?" "Of course they are. How thoughtful of you! Thank you so much," Sylvia responded, and Hilde had no choice but to ask Olga in.

Once Olga had settled in anywhere, she was very hard to get rid of, and Hilde and Sylvia were certain it would be an extremely trying afternoon. Their attention would be monopolized by Olga for hours, and their own plans no longer mattered. After grabbing some chocolate off the table, Olga got right to the point: "Does either one of you know anything about flowers," she asked, "especially showy ones like those in Zora's garden, and, of course, herbs, too? I would like to grow some in pots on the balcony and, if no one has any objections, I might even get my own little corner in our garden. I am sure you wouldn't mind although I don't know about Hans and Frieda and the rest of the neighbors."

Hilde and Sylvia were speechless. They looked at each other, astounded at Olga's unexpected interest in gardening. Maybe there is more to her than we thought, they conceded. But it was odd. Olga had never once expressed the slightest interest in beautifying her surroundings. She had never contributed to the cost of a single flower planted in the garden or done any work in it at all. So what could have possibly brought about this change? Olga did not say. How could she tell them that, not knowing the first thing about plants, her goal was to win the flower show and outdo Zora and Agnes at the same time? Or that she intended to make her own pesticides? They would no doubt burst into fits of hilarity and declare her ready for the psychiatric ward.

Reluctant to take that risk, Olga remained silent about her plans but kept pumping Hilde and Sylvia for any botanical help they might be able to provide. "Just go to a plant nursery, buy the flowers you like, stick them in the ground, fertilize them, and water them," was their advice, "and they will grow. It's no big deal." "Is that all there is to it," Olga wondered, embarrassed that she had even asked. "They must be putting me on," she decided. "It can't be that easy." But whatever it took, arduous or not, she was prepared to deal with it and promised herself she would show them in the end.

CHAPTER

T he subject of plants now having been exhausted, Sylvia and
Hilde felt that it was time for Olga to get up and make
her exit. As they had feared, however, she hung on instead,
glued to her seat. On Hilde's sideboard, she spotted a copy of the
local paper she was too stingy to buy for herself. Without asking, she
snatched it and immediately got caught up in a prominent front-
page headline that announced the arrest of teens for vandalizing city
property. Hilde who had not had time to read her own paper and
was fuming that Olga had appropriated it for herself, was suddenly
all ears when Olga identified the culprits as well as the property vandalized. And so was Sylvia. For one name stood out: Monika Berger,
Agnes's middle child.

The site she and her friends had vandalized was a unique four-
story red brick tower, part of an old spinning and weaving mill that
had recently closed but, as a listed historic landmark, had been placed
under a preservation order. A gleaming hexagonal copper dome
formed its roof, and it was on its top floor, that Monika and her
cohorts had broken the windows, sprayed graffiti all over the walls,
kicked in the doors, and left their trash and broken dishes behind.

In view of the distinctive status of the entire factory, the punishment exacted by the courts called for full restitution and hefty fines. Since the teens had no jobs and no income, however, it was their parents who were held financially responsible for the damage and had to pay up. The perpetrators themselves got off lightly because, due to their ages, they could not be held for any length of time. They were sentenced to counseling and community service and released to the custody of their parents or guardians. So, unfortunately, they would, once more, be free to shift their attention to other properties they could destroy, and the vicious cycle would begin all over again. Olga, Sylvia, and Hilde were appalled.

It crossed Olga's mind that the pleasant stranger she had seen heading for Agnes's house the day before might be connected to this incident, and she was indeed, although not as a social worker or policewoman dealing with cases of juvenile delinquency as Olga had assumed but rather as a lay sister attached to the Church of Our Dear Lady. Hilde who had met her through her work at the hospital and recognized her from Olga's description told them what she knew:

"Her name is Maria," she began, "although, when she was born, the name her parents had chosen for her was Asiye. She was raised in poverty in the stony wilderness of the Turkish mountains. Her family—including the grandparents who shared the household—was quite large but welcomed each and every addition with gratitude and joyous anticipation as there was plenty of love to go around. Asiye's traditional Moslem upbringing may have been relatively strict but it never inhibited her spirit, and she always felt treasured."

"Asiye was in her teens when she was torn out of this simple but happy life by her parents' decision to move to Germany in order to better provide for their five children. Here she felt alien and ill at ease and found it difficult to adapt to her strange new surroundings. Her two older brothers gravitated toward the Turkish community center where pleasant get-togethers and German language and karate classes were offered to the men and boys which, to a great extent, kept the latter out of trouble."

"But there was not much for the girls to do. Asiye's two sisters were too little to mind but Asiye herself felt bitterly alone without her friends. A very private person, she dreaded her German class-mates' curious eyes on her and dashed out of school as soon as it was out in the afternoons. Gradually her German improved, and, in her spare time, she took to sitting on a bench, observing the people around her."

"'Where do they go when they are down,' she asked herself. There was no Mosque anywhere but a beautiful church on the corner. The first person she saw entering through its heavy doors on a weekday was an old lady, bent from sickness and the hardships of life. But when she reappeared about ten minutes later, Asiye noticed obvious signs of relief and consolation on her previously sad face. From then on Asiye watched for her, noting that, each time she came out of the church, her burden seemed to have lightened."

"There were others, too, who obviously left their worries behind in the church, and Asiye decided to muster up the courage to check it out for herself. There she found serenity and profound calm when she needed it most. The exquisite images of the Mother of God and Baby Jesus were stretching out their arms to welcome her, and she felt at home and at peace. She loved the glow of burning candles, the aroma of holy water, and the fragrance of incense."

"From her religion classes, she knew that it was a Catholic church, not one of the Protestant churches which, she had been told, were generally starker and lacked the soothing Latin mass. And there was another reason why Asiye came to prefer Catholicism: the fact that through confession all her sins would be forgiven, and her heart would be light."

"She was hoping that that would apply to original sin as well, a concept which bothered her a lot. She strenuously objected to the idea that a pure and innocent baby could be considered guilty. To her, this was cruel and did not make sense, especially since Islam had taught her that no one shall bear the burden of another. From what she had heard and the way she understood it, no personal fault was attached to the doctrine in Catholicism whereas in the Protestant church there was no escape from its harshness, which persuaded Asiye to lean toward Catholicism even more."

"After finishing secondary school, Asiye wanted to work and live on her own. But, for a foreigner, a job was hard to come by and renting an apartment too expensive. That's when she remembered Fräulein Anni, the Catholic lay sister whom she had met at the corner church and who had offered to help her become a lay sister herself, provided she converted to Catholicism, remained celibate, and put the needs of her fellow human beings ahead of her own."

"Knowing that such a momentous step might deeply hurt her family, Asiye thought about it at length before approaching her parents with her plans. They had seen the gradual change in her and were not completely surprised but troubled and disappointed nonetheless. But love won out in the end, and they respected their daughter's decision which they were convinced she had not made lightly."

"So Asiye set out to officially become Sister Maria. When, at first, plagued by doubts, she consoled herself with the idea that there was only one God, and it didn't matter whether she called him 'Gott' or 'Allah.' She was convinced he would equally respond to either name. Comforted by this thought, she took instruction in Catholicism, psychology, and nursing, and when she had completed all her courses with distinction, she took her vows and was provided moderate quarters and a monthly allowance for food and clothing."

"Two items in her simple room reflect her heritage: on her floor, a beautiful little prayer rug given to her by her grandmother, and on her wall, an extraordinary Karagöz shadow puppet painstakingly fashioned for her out of leather by one of her uncles, a former puppeteer's apprentice with a traveling puppet theater in the Bursa area. Both the rug and the puppet delight Sister Maria whenever she looks at them, forever reminding her of her happy childhood in the remote village where she grew up and the relatives she left behind."

"I met Sister Maria when her life of serving the sick, needy, and those rejected by society had just begun. I entrusted to her care patients of mine who were alone and could not look after themselves after their discharge from the hospital. As far as I know, Sister Maria's duties also include seeking out the bedridden and frail in the community at large and aiding them in their recovery, and she is equally committed to lending a hand to the poor and those who have broken the law. Her many responsibilities keep her forever on the move, earning her genuine affection, respect, and admiration. Even her own family has come to be enormously proud of her and the huge difference she has made in people's lives, always with a smile on her face."

"Sister Maria's days are long. To fit in all of her duties, she gets up at the crack of dawn and does not get back to her room until nightfall. And even then, worrisome thoughts and concerns about all the unfortunate who so desperately need her often keep her awake. Their cries for help keep coming, even on weekends. But she does not mind her busy life. On the contrary. She feels privileged to be able to soothe her clients' discomfort and pain. It's her mission and her joy."

"Frequently unable to attend Sunday services at her church because she is needed elsewhere, Sister Maria has found a beautiful little place where she can worship on her own. You may have seen it. It looks like a tiny chapel almost hidden from view at a remote corner of The Church of Our Dear Lady. Although abutting the big church building, it is no doubt much older. The sandstone used to construct it has almost turned black with the passing of time. Its façade is simply adorned with a small rose window and molding along the eaves. There is no entrance level with the cobbled courtyard but there are stone steps that, between solid four-foot descending walls topped with pots of bright-red geraniums, lead down to a heavy wooden door with a comfortable bench beside it."

"When Sister Maria first came upon it, she was intrigued and decided to explore. She found the door unlocked, and what she discovered when she entered was an ossuary, a cave-like chamber cut into the rock, with white-washed walls and an uneven floor well below ground, its bones and skulls piled up in nooks. The door and the tiny window above it were the only sources of natural light. But a multitude of votive candles flickered in their tall red jars, all reflected in the mirror on the back wall. A delicate crucifix hung from the ceiling, and the lovely scent of holy water permeated the air."

"It was magical, and Sister Maria was entranced. This is where she wanted to worship—nowhere else. She instantly fell in love with what she now calls her little chapel, and, at sunrise every morning, she descends the steps with a flower in her hand to fill the miniature vase she found hanging on the wall and a number of candles she lights for the deceased whose bones are stored on the shelves. She says prayers for their souls and, after communing with her God in her own fashion, is invigorated and ready for work."

"How interesting, Hilde," interjected Sylvia. "Thank you for telling us about Sister Maria. I must say I have a great deal of respect for her and can't wait to meet her." And, for once, Olga agreed. "I am sure she would love to meet you, too," Hilde replied. "She is lonely. The only problem is that she does not have much time for a personal life, and if she's involved in Monika's rehabilitation, she will be even busier. But I will introduce you, I promise."

C H A P T E R

Regardless of who might be assigned to Monika's case, whether Sister Maria, a policewoman, or social worker, Olga, Hilde, and Sylvia did not envy them their job. It would be extremely difficult to exert a positive influence on an uncontrollable and defiant girl like Monika. Legal ownership meant nothing to her. She had been taught from early childhood that everything was hers for the taking or to destroy and, consequently, would allow no one, absolutely no one, to stand in her way or interfere in her life. And what was worse, she knew that, in her opposition to authority, she could count on her mother's unwavering support.

"Lost cause," remarked Olga, and, for once, Hilde agreed with her, whereas Sylvia, more magnanimous by nature, gave Monika the benefit of the doubt: "She's still young and not a hardened criminal, not yet," she said, "and there's a slight chance that someone can offer her enough patience and affection to help her turn her life around." But as much as she wanted to believe in the prospect of a normal life for Monika, even Sylvia had her reservations. It would be a tremendous challenge, too daunting to even think about after long hours in Olga's company. Exhausted, Sylvia took her leave, and Olga followed suit.

Early the next morning Olga, in fervent pursuit of her horticultural ambitions, showed up at the building's administration office to apply for her own small plot in the corner of the garden. Her request was then presented to her fellow residents for approval or rejection. Although not too fond of her, the majority saw no reason to deny it. "What's the harm," they asked themselves, "and who knows, if given a chance, she may even improve the flower beds." So, good-natured as they were, they voted in her favor.

Olga who had fully expected her wish to be granted was nevertheless gratified and busied herself immediately with bringing in all sorts of plants, fertilizer, and fresh soil. She also added so many new pots to those already on her balcony that it was almost getting too crowded for her to move around. She frequently tripped over a little shovel or rake that she had neglected to put away and kept herself from falling only by clutching at the railing. On those occasions loud clatter, muffled curses, and pitiful sighs disrupted the usual tranquility of the grounds, and everyone knew Olga had had another one of her mishaps.

During the weeks and months that Olga spent working on her plants, Sylvia showered Hilde and Fred with kindness. Hilde had finally met a man who appeared to appreciate her. He was witty and entertaining, wined and dined her, and took her for rides in his old Mercedes convertible. It was a special treat for her since she had never owned a vehicle herself and had always been dependent on public transportation. She loved feeling the breeze in her hair, was proud to be seen with him, and had a wonderful time. Hilde adored him and was ready for a commitment. She waited and waited for him to propose until she realized that the relationship was not going anywhere because he was simply enjoying his freedom. So she sent him on his way and cried her heart out on Sylvia's shoulder. Sylvia was happy to help. She was there for her friend as she was there for Fred.

Fred, too, needed her gentleness and encouragement. His wife's life was slowly ebbing away, and there was no longer anything that could be done for her. She had been in a vegetative state for years, and her physician had made it clear to Fred a long time ago that her condition was terminal. Finally having to face reality, he spent his days steeped in misery, pacing back and forth, and feeling hopeless.

It was Sylvia who pulled him out of his depression. To chase away his sadness, she suggested that he take up his old long-neglected hobbies, playing soccer and flying remote-controlled model airplanes with his pals. Once in a while, she even accompanied him to a game or a competition which gave him a solid sense of support, and on the rare occasions when he felt sufficiently at ease, he reciprocated by taking her to her favorite new-age store to pick up some incense and a crystal or two.

Zora spent the summer working in her garden and picking mushrooms and berries in the woods. On her excursions, she was often accompanied by Max who sat chattering on her shoulder or played silly games of hide-and-seek, perching motionless in the foliage of the trees and, with a cackle, challenging her to find him. It was so much fun having him with her. His amusing antics substantially relieved the hard hours of moving from location to location and all the bending, kneeling, and squatting necessary for Zora to fill her baskets.

Although she knew the forest better than anyone and was familiar with all the special places where both berries and mushrooms grew, it still took her all day to gather what she needed, and when she finally returned home with her heavy load, her back was sore, and she was exhausted. But her work was not finished. She cleaned and washed her harvest, shared it with her immediate neighbors, and made fresh egg and mushroom omelets for Adi.

On one of her trips into the woods, Zora spotted a little dog in the underbrush and, looking more closely, recognized Fluffy. He was having a great time snuffling about the hollows in the ground and completely ignored Olga who kept calling him from a short distance away. Zora approached him and, careful not to frighten him, talked to him softly and reassuringly, took hold of his collar, and gently pulled him toward Olga whom she found standing in front of a tall plant, admiring its murky-red bell-shaped flowers streaked with tinges of gold and green.

Olga had already pulled off a single blossom and held it up to her nose to determine its smell, good or bad. Disappointed, she then had focused her attention on the shiny black berries, each rising from a star-shaped calyx. And just as she was reaching for one of them, Zora uttered a cry of caution. Olga was so startled that she flinched and dropped Fluffy's leash. Annoyed with Zora for causing her to lose her composure, she demanded an immediate explanation.

As Zora identified the plant as deadly nightshade and threw light on its extremely poisonous properties, Olga's anger slowly faded away. She began to appreciate the danger she had been in, and her heart was filled with gratitude. "Thank you, Zora," she managed to stammer, "you may have saved my life," and, humbled, she headed home with Fluffy in tow.

Clearly, learning how to garden turned out to be a haphazard process for Olga who experienced many failures and few successes along the way. She visited all the nurseries in town to see what was blooming and which plants might be best suited for her purpose, and yet she never bought any of them. Instead she walked through various neighborhoods with a big bag on her arm, cut off the flowers she thought she could root herself, and pulled out others she liked with their roots intact when the ground was wet after a soaking rain. With practice, Olga became a deft hand at never staying in one location for very long, hiding behind fences and bushes, quickly stepping out to pinch a twig, and dropping it into her bag. To all appearances innocent, she then returned home with a bagful of plunder.

Olga's flower bed was nothing to brag about. It had turned into a motley of weeds and blossoms and dead and live plants partially sapped by aphids and mold. In hindsight her neighbors were questioning the wisdom of letting Olga have her own plot. But careful not to antagonize her with negative comments, they went out of their way to praise her efforts whenever they saw her working in the garden. They gave her credit for trying and were quite willing to be patient with her until she could gain more experience.

"She has probably bitten off more than she can chew," they acknowledged, keeping in mind Olga's tending to an entirely different set of plants on her balcony at the same time, not the showy flowers she was planning to grow in the garden but herbs and seed-lings she nurtured for future use in home-made insecticides. "The ants and wasps and, lately, the spiders, too, may have been given a reprieve but I will get them in the end," Olga vowed.

On weekends, Olga took time off from her plants to visit her family grave and water it if necessary. She loved the serenity and quiet of the Cemetery of the Church of Peace and the singing of the many birds that had made it their home. The cemetery consisted of two parts, the original graveyard and the relatively new area, the resting place of fallen soldiers, marked only with wooden crosses and planted with tulips and forget-me-nots.

It was the old section that Olga liked. She never tired of walking up and down the pebbled paths, past granite slabs, mossy tombstones, and ornate crypts, trying to decipher faded inscriptions obscured by the huge branches of ancient yews, or resting under a clump of weep-ing birches. Each burial plot was different. Some were almost bare although the majority were filled with a profusion of flowers.

C H A P T E R

19

Olga considered the cemetery her personal retreat that belonged to no one but her, especially in the early morning hours when it was nearly deserted. She then had it all to herself, except for Liesl who seemed to be everywhere regardless of the time of day. To Olga, she was a nuisance, always hanging about, when in reality Liesl was only doing her job.

As the general factotum of the cemetery, Liesl worked tirelessly. She went from grave to grave to find the many flowers that were hanging their heads, especially during the hot summer months. She made endless trips to the fountain where she took one of the green watering cans off the hook, filled it with water, and laboriously carried it to where it was needed, no easy task for someone as slight as Liesl. For the cans were big and, filled to the top, almost too heavy for her. Once the flowers had been watered, Liesl often bent down and talked to them, encouraging them to stay healthy and delight the dead and living alike with their blooms.

Liesl also pulled weeds but never without an apology for depriving them of life. Only thistles were safe from being discarded. For Liesl loved them and, instead of taking them to the compost pile, moved them to less conspicuous places.

In the winter, Liesl cleared the walkways of ice and snow so none of the visitors would come to harm, took care of the seedlings in her little greenhouse, and made sure the birds had enough to eat. She knew them all, had baptized them in her mind, and called them by name. She chatted with them whenever she could, and they responded with tweets, chirps, and warbles, and sometimes even a beautiful song.

A shrewd observer, Liesl knew that trying to please people like Olga meant fighting a losing battle. Olga had never had a kind word for her. On the contrary. All she did was criticize and treat Liesl like an underling who had nothing to do but comply with her demands. Although very well aware that pets were not allowed in the cemetery, Olga always brought Fluffy inside instead of tying him to the fence at the entrance as other dog owners did as a matter of course. It was not Fluffy's presence, however, that angered Liesl. It was the disgusting piles he deposited which Olga conveniently ignored, and Liesl was left to clean up.

By nature positive and upbeat, Liesl was determined not to allow Olga's obvious disrespect for her to ruin her day. She was deeply hurt by it but, as usual, preferred to look on the bright side: Olga was one of a kind whose small-mindedness and nasty barbs could never over-shadow the kindness and appreciation Liesl saw in the smiling faces of the other cemetery visitors every day.

Liesl was in her early thirties and instantly recognizable by the colorful pinafores she wore over her outfits. Short and skinny, she had a pretty oval-shaped face. Her thick chestnut hair was gathered in a shiny braid that hung down her back, and a sea of freckles covered her small pug nose and the top of her ruddy cheeks, one of which was slightly marked by three or four short and narrow scars that had been inflicted by a stray kitten when she was a toddler.

Liesl was the only child of Hedwig who had died when she was born and Leo, the cemetery custodian. All she knew of her mother was that she had been a seamstress and had made the tastiest sauerbraten in the world. When she passed away so unexpectedly, Leo was devastated and made a solemn promise to himself that he would be the best father ever to the tiny sweet baby for whom his wife had sacrificed her life. It was a promise he was to keep faithfully and unwaveringly as long as he lived.

Liesl thrived under his loving care and guidance. As soon as she learned to walk, she started following her father wherever he went in the cemetery, trying to help him with his chores. And although she occasionally slowed down his work, Leo always remained patient. Hurting Liesl's feelings would have been unthinkable so he never let on that sometimes she was in the way. He talked to her gently and kindly, teaching her quite a bit about keeping the flowers alive and the cemetery clean and neat during her preschool years.

By the age of six, Liesl had become a spirited little girl with sparkling green eyes and a mischievous grin. She was sharp and did well in school but was easily bored. So used to being free to move around, it was hard for her to sit still, and she terribly missed spending her days with her father. When she finally completed her mandatory education, she was determined to follow in his footsteps and would consider neither occupational training nor studying at the local university.

Knowing how very bright Liesl was, Leo was conflicted. On the one hand, he was disappointed that she refused to continue her education; on the other, he felt that Liesl's happiness mattered much more than her standing in society ever would. At the same time, he was so very proud, deeply touched, and overjoyed that she would choose being with him and taking care of the cemetery over any potential advancement that might have come her way.

Finished with school, Liesl was elated and could not stop smiling. She finally had her life back. To her the cemetery with its beautiful flowers and lively birds was a paradise, quiet and serene, never disrupted by strict teachers or loud boys and girls. Its peace made her spirit soar, and all the boredom she had suffered in school was forgotten.

The cemetery with its wonderful flora, birdsong, and fascinating grave markers became Liesl's sanctuary and maintaining it her purpose in life. For years, she devotedly assisted her father, and when Leo died after decades of faithful and dedicated service, Liesl was allowed to stay on and continue occupying the small annex on cemetery grounds where her family had always lived—a decision no one had ever regretted.

For her efforts, Liesl was paid very little. But she was happy. She was frugal, did not need a great deal, and did not have to pay rent. She readily adopted the graves of the old and feeble when they could no longer take care of them and, as a token of their gratitude, sometimes received a few groceries or a small amount of money in return. Liesl was absolutely trustworthy, and when she made a promise, she kept it.

CHAPTER

One day Liesl observed a curious incident: Olga, as she
often did, was sitting on a bench with Fluffy on her lap.
Through a hole in the shrub Liesl was getting ready to clip,
she watched Olga riveting her eyes on an old family mausoleum a
short distance away, setting Fluffy down, and walking up to the large
tombstone fronting its entrance. "It's an interesting memorial," Liesl
was thinking, "and I don't blame Frau Lindermann for wanting to
check it out."

But evidently that was not Olga's intention at all. A minute or
so later, she turned up with something resembling a bouquet in her
hand, before disappearing from Liesl's field of vision again. "What's
Frau Lindermann doing," Liesl wondered when she heard a muffled
but undoubtedly heated argument erupt between a male and someone who sounded like Olga on the other side of the hedge. "Strange,"
Liesl reflected. But it was none of her business, and she had to get
back to work.

To Liesl the incident was to remain a mystery. What she had
not been able to discern from her vantage point was that, from her
place on the bench, Olga had caught sight of the biggest and most
exquisite blossoms she had ever seen. They adorned the façade of the

mausoleum, and Olga could not wait to identify them. Her glasses did not seem to help so she put Fluffy on his leash and dragged him toward the plant to get a closer look. Even then, she did not recognize the tall shrub bearing the beautiful huge reddish-purple flowers. Their size and shape, however, did ring a bell. She remembered seeing similar creamy yellow ones in one of the library books. The name "datura" or "angel's trumpet" came to mind, and she was determined to read up on it when she got home. Only this seemed to be a rare color, not the common yellow, and Olga could not resist. Convinced she would not be able to find it elsewhere, she looked around furtively and swiftly took a few cuttings, thinking that the dead certainly would not mind.

"Caught you, didn't I—stealing from the dead! Shame on you, you old cow! I must say, you photograph well! Want to see?" And Fabian stepped out of the shadows, holding out his camera to her. Olga was mortified when she actually saw herself on the screen. There was no doubt. It was proof of her guilt. "I suppose you want me to get rid of this picture," Fabian continued. "What is it worth to you if I do? Fifty marks to start with should do it, or you might find yourself in the paper tomorrow. Not so haughty now, are you, "Fräulein" Lindermann?"

Hearing herself addressed as "Fräulein," not as "Frau"—the title of respect women of a certain age had a right to, even if not married—and especially Fabian's deliberate emphasis on it, made Olga quake with indignation and rage. In her eyes, it was an intentional insult by a good-for-nothing louse who, to top it all, dared to blackmail her, the upstanding citizen she had always considered herself to be. "There must be something I can do," she thought. But nothing came to mind. Olga knew she was cornered. She was desperately trying to keep a brave face but her hands gave away her fear. They were trembling so severely that, although barely managing to hold on to Fluffy's leash, Olga dropped her purse.

"How come you have the shakes? Did I do that to you," Fabian taunted her. "Why don't I help you pick up your bag?" Olga bent down to get to it first but Fabian was too fast. He quickly moved toward her, bumped into her, almost knocking her off her feet, grabbed the purse, and started rummaging through it. With a mocking expression on his face, he carelessly scattered her belongings until he found her leather wallet.

"Well, well, old bat, let's see if this keeps your picture out of the paper," he said and opened it, to discover only one five-mark note and a number of coins. "You can't be serious. This is ridiculous. Where is your money? Don't tell me this is all you have. I know better. So where is it? Tell me right now, or tomorrow you will be the laughing stock of the town," he threatened. Olga, beaten-down and seeing no other way out, admitted having some notes stashed away in a zip-up side pocket for emergencies only. It did not take Fabian long to find them. He triumphantly held up fifty marks and put them in his pocket. The rest of the money he put back, warning Olga not to spend it as he might have use for it in the future.

Then Fabian was gone, vanished behind the mausoleum. Olga looked around, relieved that no one had come along to witness the embarrassing scene. But then she was in an older and fairly remote area of the cemetery that did not get many visitors. In that respect, Olga had been lucky. But she was still trembling from fright and the menace that Fabian represented. "Odious creature," she said to herself, "make no mistake, you will pay for this."

She tied Fluffy's leash to a tree, picked up her glasses that she had dropped in the scuffle, and set out to gather the items from her purse that Fabian had deliberately tossed on the ground. Her anger and panic having somewhat abated, she led Fluffy back to the bench where they had earlier enjoyed a peaceful afternoon. She sat down, put Fluffy on her lap, tried to compose herself and collect her thoughts in an attempt to weigh her options. But she was still much too emotional to deal logically with this problem that had suddenly taken over her life.

Two weeks later, Fabian was back. This time he stepped out from behind a bush in the park, just after one of Olga's typical altercations with another dog owner. Olga was already agitated enough, and seeing Fabian emerge to disrupt her otherwise fairly normal day really ignited her fury. "Leave me alone, you sorry excuse for a human being," she screamed but was quickly silenced by his flashing the picture he had taken in the cemetery and the malevolent grin on his face.

"What if I were to convince him that there is nothing left for him to extort," she wondered. "Would that get rid of him? It might just be worth a try," and in an attempt to appeal to his sense of compassion, she begged: "Fabian, please, you know that I am an old woman retired from my job. My pension is just enough for me to live on and feed Fluffy. I really don't have anything to spare, and I am sure you wouldn't want us to go hungry, would you?" Fabian was quick to respond: "Boohoo! Thought you could fool me? I know all about your circumstances. Your stinginess is legendary. No one expects a tip or a donation from you no matter how badly they need it, and now you even resort to stealing to save a few pennies here and a few pennies there and put yourself on easy street. You make me sick! I have no sympathy for you. It's your turn to give, and give you will—to me. Another fifty, or your name will be mud!"

This was just what Olga dreaded the most: being humiliated in public and having her pride crushed. She would never be able to show her face again. So she grudgingly reached into her purse, pulled out a fifty-mark note and handed it to Fabian who jerked it out of her hand and took off, sniggering loudly. Somebody must have told him that I don't give tips or support beggars, Olga reflected. It had to have been his mother, she decided, and her loathing of Agnes intensified. What kinds of people are these, she asked herself. Who keeps hiding empty wine bottles under the broken furniture in the yard? No wonder the father moved out. He has always been a decent person about whom nothing negative is known. And what's Simon's role in all this? Is he equally delinquent or does he just tolerate his younger siblings' depravity, and maybe his mother's, too?

CHAPTER

Although temporarily distracted by Agnes and her children, Olga's thoughts always reverted to her own situation with a pang. Olga was rattled to the core. She knew Fabian would return and squeeze her dry. She saw his face everywhere and felt haunted. She made a tremendous effort to clear her brain and come up with promising ways of dealing with her blackmailer. Turning him in to the police would make the most sense. But they would find out that she stole the flowers, and a police report might end up in the paper after all. So that was out. It would be too demeaning. She could possibly talk to Philipp, Fabian's father. But regardless of his child's character, wouldn't a parent always stick up for his son? And talking to Agnes, Olga knew, would be equally useless since she and Fabian were most likely partners in crime.

So what was left for her to do? She could keep paying Fabian, which was unthinkable. She could confront him and threaten him with prosecution but that would hardly worry anyone as hard-boiled as Fabian since legally he was still a minor and undoubtedly knew there would be no serious consequences. Olga briefly thought of confiding in Sister Maria whom she liked and who, as a lay sister, would keep their conversation confidential and perhaps provide some valuable advice. But Olga was not ready to confess, and, just for a second, a fleeting thought crossed her mind, making a connection between her poisonous plants and eliminating Fabian herself.

During the next few days, Olga pondered these possibilities over and over again. There was no room for much else in her mind. The threat of being exposed by Fabian kept her awake at night, and she was deeply troubled until she decided to face her dilemma head-on. What's so reprehensible about what I have done, she asked herself. It's not that I have hurt someone or robbed a bank. What am I really guilty of? Picking a few flowers—so what? Maybe getting them at the cemetery was not a good idea and would give some people the wrong impression since supposedly it's sacred ground. But otherwise I'm blameless, and no vicious punk can change that. I have my self-respect and will not be dragged into the gutter by anyone, least of all Fabian. So he had better watch out.

Having assessed her situation, Olga experienced some relief, especially since there had been no sign of Fabian in quite a while, and her fears were easing. She was sure he had other victims, and maybe one of them had proven to be such a good source of funds that he did not need her any longer. So her guard was down when he raised his ugly head once again and startled her one day, just as she was badgering another homeless man, one of her favorite targets, on market square. Fabian unexpectedly walked up behind her, got really close, and in a low but determined voice and in no uncertain terms ordered her to give the beggar at least ten marks and hand over a fifty to him. To avoid a scene, Olga complied. The poor recipient was incredulous at her uncharacteristic benevolence and Fabian disappeared into the crowd.

So he's back after all. I had a feeling he would be, Olga sighed. She bitterly resented the entire world for having singled her out as Fabian's prey. The sunshine and the flowers that had never failed to lift her spirits had vanished. It was beginning to rain, and the temperature was dropping. Summer had turned into fall. The wind was picking up, and Olga was chilled to the bone. The blooms are all fading, she realized, and tears were running down her cheeks. "My plants are dying, and I have nothing left, except for you," she said to

Fluffy, picked him up and gave him a hug. "We'll get through the winter together and keep each other warm."

When she stepped into her living room, she saw one bright spot in the relative darkness: the periwinkle-blue flowers of an African violet on her window sill, a recent gift from Sylvia. It was a ray of hope, beautiful and in full bloom. It reminded her of her neighbor's kindness and gave her some reassurance that she might not be completely alone after all. But she could not shake off the shadow Fabian had cast over her life.

She sat in the dark for hours, oblivious to her surroundings, wondering what to do until Fluffy started whining and tugged at her sleeve. She reluctantly allowed him to pull her toward the bedroom. It was almost midnight. Neither of them had had any dinner and, while Fluffy slept soundly, Olga was plagued by thoughts of unpleasant scenarios involving Fabian and dozing only periodically and fitfully until the next morning when Fluffy stood there bright-eyed and bushy-tailed, and Olga was too exhausted to move.

For now, the most elusive thought floating at the edge of Olga's consciousness, of perhaps getting rid of Fabian by means of toxic plants, had receded into the background. There were no plants during the cold season that she would have been able to use anyway. So for the time being, Olga's hands were tied. She remained inert and fell into a deep depression.

No more daily shopping for her. Always a welcome diversion in the past, it had become too much of a chore which she could now endure only once a week if at all. She no longer took Fluffy for his regular walks in the park but merely carried him downstairs for a few minutes whenever he had to go, not only to stay out of Fabian's reach but also to avoid the other dog owners. The confrontations with them she had always enjoyed had lost their appeal, and instead of looking forward to them as she previously had, she had taken to glancing nervously all around her and, whenever she saw someone approaching from afar, hurriedly pulled Fluffy in the opposite direction, anxious to get away. She had become jittery and easily spooked and flinched when unexpectedly spoken to.

Her appearance, too, had suffered. Olga, ordinarily so meticulous about her looks, now often walked around unkempt, in wrinkled clothing, her treasured high heels replaced by old, worn-out flats. She no longer bothered to dye her hair, and gray patches started to infiltrate her previously carefully maintained reddish-brown bob. There were dark rings around her eyes, her face was covered with blotches, and there was no trace of lipstick. She had aged rapidly and looked disheveled and sad.

Olga was in no mood to prepare either her garden plot or her balcony for the winter. The plants, at least those that were still living, seemed to reflect her state of mind. None of them had been trimmed or covered up to protect them from the coming cold. Pots were standing around everywhere, and the weeds were thriving. To the neighbors, her flower bed was an eyesore, and many were wondering what had happened to her. She had never been an accomplished gardener but at least she used to have the willingness and enthusiasm to make an effort. But now everything had fallen into neglect.

Frequently, even Fluffy's needs were ignored by Olga. Whenever she forgot to feed him and inadvertently left the door ajar, he came to Sylvia's or Hilde's flat, whimpering and begging for food. They knew he meant everything to Olga and were at a loss to explain her apparent indifference. Both began to stock dog biscuits in their pantries although the old Olga would definitely have preferred fresh cuts of meat for her pet. These neither of them could afford but they were doing the best they could under the circumstances. Sometimes they even took Fluffy for a walk and let him play in the snow. Hans and Frieda, too, pitched in by setting out water and dog food for Fluffy at the bottom of the stairs.

While Olga remained paralyzed with fear and depression, the theft of Zora's coin was finally solved, in part by a little boy who had come into the park with a sack of bread crumbs for the ducks. While talking to them, he observed Zora's crow digging in the fork of some tree branches, retrieving a small item, and getting ready to fly off with it in his beak. When the sunlight hit it, it glinted and really caught his eye. He was curious and, knowing Max well, followed him home to Zora's house and arrived at a moment of great happiness when Zora had just recognized her coin and broken into a song. She welcomed the little boy, listened to his story, and gave him a piece of his favorite chocolate. Then she reported the return of her gold coin to the authorities.

Two police officers went to the park to check out the place where Max had picked it up to determine whether it had been left there by the bird himself, only to be retrieved by him later, or whether it was a thief who had done so. What they discovered was a cut obviously made with a knife that had held the coin in place. So they decided to take turns, inconspicuously watching the tree in case the perpetrator showed up to claim his prize.

Endless hours and days went by until finally someone approached the tree, opened a folding chair, stepped on it, and reached for the coin. It was Agnes dressed in old clothing, her face partially hidden by a large shawl that fell over her shoulders. When she was identified, she came apart at the seams. She broke down crying as if her world had come to an end, repeating over and over that the coin was the only thing she had ever possessed that was exclusively her own.

Agnes eventually confessed. It turned out that one night when she was spying on her neighbors during a drunken stroll, she saw Zora looking at her coin by candlelight, thought it quite beautiful, and immediately made up her mind to claim it for herself. So one day when Zora was gone, and Agnes found her door unlocked, she went in, grabbed it, and hid it in the tree to keep it safe from her children.

The consequences of this theft for Agnes were not particularly harsh. Having her coin back was all that mattered to Zora, and she, therefore, refrained from pressing charges. The only punishment Agnes faced were probation and a considerable fine. It could have been much worse for her but this being her first known offense as well as her family's standing in the community accounted for the leniency of the court.

C H A P T E R

Olga did not find out about this development until much later. She remained in isolation the entire winter, and the neighbors hardly ever caught a glimpse of her. On the few occasions when they did see her, she refused to speak to them. They had no idea what was going on with her but, convinced that something was terribly wrong, they were deeply worried. After months of witnessing Olga's deterioration, Sylvia and Hilde finally decided to do something about it. Sylvia had already written, and slid under Olga's door, numerous warm-hearted notes offering her assistance but Olga had not acknowledged any of them. It occurred to Hilde that Sister Maria might be the perfect person to consult, and Sylvia agreed to enlist her help.

Sister Maria was happy to intervene. She knocked several times before Olga finally came to the door. Her face lit up when she recognized Sister Maria who was pleasantly surprised at the cordial reception as she had fully expected to be turned away. But, by now, Olga had become so desperate that she needed to confess, even if that meant swallowing her pride. And there was no one she would rather unburden herself to than Sister Maria. She knew that anything she said would be kept in strict confidence, and that there would be no repercussions of any kind. So she told Sister Maria about her habit of raiding gardens and Fabian's catching her cutting a few flowers at the cemetery, taking a picture of her in the process, and blackmailing her ever since.

"Stealing flowers is not a mortal sin," Sister Maria tried to console her, "but I know that is not what you are worried about. What troubles you more than anything, I think, is that other people might find out what you have done. It would be a serious blow to your self-esteem. You are terrified that you might be tarnished in their eyes and that, when you interact with them, they will see you as somehow diminished and no longer blemish-free, and all their respect for you will have evaporated. You are too proud for your own good."

"Our conversation is confidential so no one will learn about your theft unless you tell them yourself which may not be such a bad idea. But it should be your decision. You could admit to your transgression and jokingly refer to it as a temporary aberration. Your neighbors probably already have an idea of where you might have gotten your plants. Just laugh about it with them, and they will appreciate you more for being human and honest than for portraying the perfect and inanimate image as you have attempted to do. Think about it! A little humility has never hurt anyone."

"But if that option is too daunting for you or seems too hasty, you could always seek forgiveness at home or in church. Since you are not Catholic, you cannot go to formal confession although, if it's meaningful to you, you can always ask God for absolution on your own. It may make you feel better about yourself. Also, if you ever see another beautiful flower that you would like to have or grow, why not just ring the doorbell and ask for permission to take one or two cuttings. People love to have their gardens noticed and admired, and may be so pleased by your request that they will give you entire plants including their roots. It's always worth a try."

"It's obvious you don't want a lecture and that's what you have been getting from me. I am sorry. I know what you do want is a real solution to your problem, escaping from Fabian's clutches without losing face, and on that front, I have good news. Fabian will not bother you again. He was recently picked up for fraud after numerous complaints had been received, mostly from seniors and disabled citizens who cannot, or are struggling to, walk, all asserting that a young man had offered to make purchases for them, and, instead of coming back with the items on their shopping lists, had absconded with their money."

"In the beginning, no one knew who he was so the police conducted a sting operation in front of the main shopping center, with an undercover officer impersonating an old man in a wheelchair. Fabian fell into the trap, and every one of the victims, without exception, identified him as the perpetrator. There is absolutely no doubt about his guilt. He is currently in custody and will be put away for some time."

Olga who had not uttered a single word now broke down in tears, releasing the misery she had suffered for almost an entire, very long year. She still could not quite grasp the fact that she was finally free but gradually, as she started to comprehend her rescue, a few timid smiles began to mingle with her sobs. She was hugely relieved. Sister Maria had saved her life. For joy, anyone but Olga might have sung a happy tune. Not Olga. She did not have a musical bone in her body.

When told that it was Hilde and Sylvia who had sought Sister Maria's assistance on her behalf, Olga was so pleased that her neighbors had cared enough to help her, she resolved to reward them for their kindness. For Sister Maria, she brewed fresh coffee and warmed up some croissants over which they lingered until Olga's equanimity had been fully restored.

That night, Olga's sleep was sound and undisturbed, and, when the sunshine lighting up her room finally woke her, she could not stop smiling. She stepped out onto her balcony and took deep breaths. The air was fresh and cool, and the birds were singing. Spring had come. Olga looked down on the park and saw a galaxy of dewdrops sparkling in the sun. A number of daisies and cowslips were blooming in the meadow, and snowdrops were raising their heads in a grassless spot. The deciduous trees had acquired faint traces of color from a multitude of yellowish, lime-green, and reddish buds. "How beautiful it all is," Olga exclaimed and fetched Fluffy to show him the lovely view. He, too, had slept soundly, perhaps sensing the peace in Olga's heart.

After breakfast, Olga dressed most carefully. She put on lipstick and some blush and covered up her mottled hair with one of her fancy hats, reminding herself to stop by the drugstore to purchase some dye. She threw her old flats in the back of her closet and painstakingly chose a pair of high heels to go with her favorite gray suit. A dark-blue cardigan completed her outfit. Fluffy, too, got to wear one of his best ensembles so laboriously created by Hilde, and off they went, first through the park, exchanging greetings with other dog owners and their pets, and then toward town.

Olga's destination was a gift shop that she had frequented since her childhood, not always to buy something but often just to look. Peter, the current owner, whose grandfather had founded the business, was Olga's contemporary. Like all men in his family, he was a master glass blower by profession, and his shop was full of amazing and colorful works of his art, sparkling in the light. There were all sorts of little people, fairy tale characters, animals, flowers, paperweights, and marbles—a paradise, especially for children. Each figurine was unique, and no two were alike.

For once, Olga had decided to spend money, not on herself, but on Hilde and Sylvia who had been so supportive during her time of anguish. If she had been honest with herself or examined her motives, however, she might have realized that she was not buying presents for them out of love or gratitude or just to make them happy, but rather to show the world that she paid her debts. She knew very well what was seemly and expected and would rather have died than being seen as stingy, unappreciative, or unrefined. Appearances, after all, mattered a great deal.

Selecting suitable gifts, for Olga, was a matter of pride. Finding the perfect one for Sylvia was easy. It was prominently displayed, and Olga spotted it immediately. It was a delicate little angel in a white lace dress which reminded Olga of a fine-textured frock in Sylvia's wardrobe. The angel had soft green wings, a pink flower in its pale-yellow hair, and a smile on its face.

Hilde's present took Olga a bit longer to find. Whereas Sylvia was fond of pastel colors, Olga knew that Hilde preferred bright and vibrant hues. But what type of figurine would she like, Olga asked herself. Unlike Sylvia, Hilde did not collect angels; she had no pets, and a flower might be too impersonal. So what was left? She kept looking at the wonderful selection in front of her until her eyes alighted on a little nurse with a red cross on her white cap. The figurine was wearing a simple lemon top over a brown skirt sprinkled with a profusion of multicolored blossoms. Olga was thrilled. She had no doubt that Hilde, being a nurse's aide, would love it.

On the way to the cash register to pay for her gifts, Olga detected a little glass dog that was the spitting image of Fluffy. She could not take her eyes off it and was so excited that she pointed out to Peter its resemblance to her pet who, at the moment, was tied to a lamppost outside. Discerning Olga's joy, Peter picked up the figurine and put it in her pocket. "No charge," he said, and Olga was over the moon, profusely thanking Peter for his kindness.

Somehow Peter's generous gesture made her think of the kindness Zora had shown her on several occasions and, to Olga's shame and regret, had remained unreciprocated. Maybe I can find a small present for Zora, too, Olga told herself and again viewed Peter's delightful inventory until she discovered a little black crow that looked exactly like Max. "I have found it," she happily informed Peter and added the bird to her purchases. "It's perfect, and I can't tell you how pleased I am," she continued and proceeded to settle her bill.

Back home, Olga wrapped Sylvia's and Hilde's figurines in tissue paper and tied the tops with ribbons saved from gifts given to her in the past. Pleased with her efforts, she called Hilde to find out when it would be convenient to see both her and Sylvia together. At the appointed time, Olga went down, knocked on Hilde's door, and was greeted by her neighbors with welcome compliments on her appearance, having suddenly changed from that of a bag lady to one of gentility.

"What happened to you," they asked in unison. "It was Sister Maria's visit that solved all my problems," Olga told them, "and I so much appreciate your sending her to me. That's why I have brought you little tokens of my gratitude," she added, handing them their presents. They were received with surprise, on the one hand, since Olga had never given them anything before, and great delight, on the other. As the figurines were unwrapped, their beauty emerged, and both Hilde and Sylvia were full of admiration for Peter's artistry. They could not have imagined prettier or more fitting gifts and praised Olga for the perfect choices she had made. Each loved her own figurine and vowed to give it a place of honor in her flat.

"I am so happy you like your presents," Olga continued, "but I have come not only as a bearer of gifts but also one of good news. Imagine, Fabian is locked up, and we can all breathe a sigh of relief." She told them about the crimes that landed Fabian behind bars but did not disclose any connection between him and her predicament. It would have meant admitting to the ignominious part she played by stealing the flowers. She was not ready for that, which left her neighbors completely in the dark as to what had happened to her. What could have led up to such a low point in Olga's life in the first place, they wondered, and how was she able to finally overcome it? All they knew was that it had something to do with Sister Maria.

Reluctant to satisfy their curiosity by asking unwanted and intrusive questions, Sylvia and Hilde tactfully steered the conversation to Sister Maria's good deeds until it occurred to Sylvia that Hans and Frieda, too, deserved recognition for setting out food and water for Fluffy when Olga was unable to do so herself. Aware of the friction between Frieda and Olga, Sylvia hoped to smooth the waters by bringing Hans and Frieda's generosity to Olga's attention, and when she did, Olga had a hard time holding back tears. Profoundly touched by the realization that no one had let her down when she needed them most, she, then and there, decided to reward Sister Maria as well as Hans and Frieda with beautiful figurines of their own.

The next day Olga was back at the gift shop. "Nice to see you again so soon," Peter greeted her at the door. "Is there anything I can help you with?" "Well, Peter," replied Olga, "I need three more figurines. One should definitely be a nun and the others something for an older couple. "At the moment there are no religious items on display," said Peter, "but I may have one or two in the back." And luckily he did. He returned with a little nun, wearing a black habit with a white scapular over it, tiny rosary beads hanging from her belt, a white wimple and black veil, and a silver cross on her chest. Her sweet face immediately appealed to Olga who, convinced that Sister Maria would love her gift as soon as she saw it, put it in her basket.

The selection of Hans and Frieda's presents proved to be rather more difficult. What do you give acquaintances you are not really close to, Olga pondered. While reflecting on her neighbors' possible likes and dislikes, she kept scanning the shelves but could not come to a decision until it occurred to her that Hans and Frieda's grandchildren meant more to them than anything else in the world. They adored them and spoiled them immensely.

That's the answer, Olga congratulated herself, relieved. I will get figurines for the children instead. From Peter's storybook characters, she selected Hänsel for the little boy and Gretel for the little girl. Hänsel's outfit consisted of long green pants, a blue shirt, and a red pointed hat, and Gretel was dressed in a colorful flowered skirt, a pink top, and a yellow cap over her braids. They looked quite impish and ready for adventure, and Olga found them adorable. "They are just what I had in mind," she said. "Thank you, Peter, for your help. My purchases are complete." She paid for them, untied Fluffy from the lamppost, and headed for home, anxious to wrap and deliver her presents.

In view of their quarrel about the existence or non-existence of Olga's fiancé, Hans and Frieda were at first rather distant although perfectly polite when Olga rang their doorbell. They expected trouble but Olga's friendliness put them at ease, and she was invited in. There were pictures of the grandchildren everywhere, and Olga knew she could not have picked better gifts. She acknowledged the kindness Hans and Frieda had shown her and Fluffy during her difficult time and handed Hänsel to Hans and Gretel to Frieda.

They all laughed when the figurines were unwrapped. "So you bought us fairy tale characters at our age," Frieda teased Olga. "No, of course not," she responded. "I couldn't think of anything you needed so I got these for your grandchildren." "They are wonderful," Hans said, "and will delight the little ones. They are deeply appreciated by all of us." There were smiles all around, and peace among the neighbors was reestablished.

Next on Olga's delivery list was Sister Maria. She set out with Fluffy for the Church of Our Dear Lady but, not exactly sure where Sister Maria lived and in doubt whether she would have access to her flat anyway, she stopped by the church office to inquire. It turned out that Sister Maria was out on a job so Olga wrote a note and left her gift with the secretary who sent her on her way with thanks, a blessing, and good wishes.

Now comes the most difficult delivery, Olga realized, pondering the difference in social standing between Zora and herself, Zora's kindness, and her own lack of response. Zora was wary and, like Hans and Frieda, expected trouble when she saw Olga and Fluffy at the gate.

"Don't worry, Zora," Olga calmed her, "I am not here to bother you, just to admire your spring flowers and thank you for being so good and helpful to me in the past. I know it's been a long time but please forgive the delay and accept the little gift I have brought you as an expression of my gratitude." Adding "I hope you like it," she handed Zora the figurine. "Like is not the word for it," responded Zora after unwrapping her gift. "I love it! It's my Max immortalized in glass! How lifelike he is, and he does have a lot of character. Thank you so much."

Although still not entirely comfortable with Zora, Olga was pleased and relieved that their talk had been so amicable. The gnawing sensation of indebtedness that had plagued her for some time was finally gone. Her presents had made up for her neighbors' acts of kindness, and her self-esteem had rallied considerably. Content, she returned to her flat.

CHAPTER

24

There was one person, however, whose work on her behalf Olga had neglected to acknowledge, perhaps because she hovered at the periphery of Olga's lofty world and, therefore, for her, barely existed. It was Liesl who had kept Olga's grave free of snow and ice and her perennials protected from the cold all winter. Liesl would have been happy with a brief "thank you," even if grudgingly said, but then she had never expected any recognition from Olga at all and was not surprised when it did not come. Liesl had done her duty, felt good about helping someone out, even if it was Olga, and saw no reason to question Olga's long absence or apparent failure to face up to her responsibilities. It meant more work for her, to be sure, but, more importantly, it also meant peace of mind.

While Liesl dreaded Olga's reappearance, she always looked forward to seeing the poor homeless who came into the cemetery to rest on its comfortable benches during opening hours. So unlike difficult, ungrateful, and hostile Olga, they were friendly and humble and appreciated everything Liesl did for them. She listened to their stories with compassion and, if warranted, enlisted Sister Maria whom she had met in church to look after their needs. Whenever they were hungry or thirsty, she provided food and drink from her own pantry so they would not have to suffer. She also collected blankets, clothing, and shoes for them among the families of the recently deceased who were only too happy to find good use for the items no longer needed by their loved ones.

Soon after the death of Liesl's father, a new homeless man had appeared at the cemetery, and Liesl had taken to him immediately. He was younger than most of his comrades, roughly her age, and looked at her with a big grin on his face. He was fairly tall and so thin that his tattered clothes looked like they could have accommodated a second person of his build. Liesl sensed that, in spite of the circumstances he found himself in, he was basically a happy soul. He had big wide-spaced gray eyes and a mop of orangey hair frequently hidden under a grass-green knitted cap. Liesl noticed how clean he was and suspected that he took advantage of the public showers at the train station.

Of course, she was curious. Who could he be and how did he get into his current predicament, she wondered. So, after exchanging greetings with him a few times, she sat down next to him, introduced herself, and initiated a conversation, gently prodding him to tell her about himself. His name was Ulli, and his story was sad: When he was nineteen years old, while apprenticed to his father, a chimney sweep, he had fallen off a roof and seriously injured himself. When it was determined that the head trauma he had suffered had left him unable to continue his training, his father had made it clear to him that he was no longer of any use to him or his business and kicked him out. His mother, a downtrodden woman, had no say in the matter. She loved Ulli and hated her husband for being so cruel. Vowing to rescue her from her abuser one day, Ulli left his childhood home with nothing but his harmonica, to live on the streets.

To support himself, Ulli did a little busking and joined a village band that played not only on special occasions but also every Saturday under a very old, majestic linden tree from the base of which a scaffold-like structure led up to a wooden platform that served as a dance floor. Ulli had so much fun playing his harmonica there and was so good at it that people loved to listen to his music and were quite generous with their tips. These supplemented the small disability check he received from the government each month but did not add up to enough to put a roof over his head. He did not mind, however. He loved nature, and he loved to be free, not beholden to anyone.

Slowly Liesl and Ulli became friends. She occasionally invited him to her home, the small bungalow on cemetery grounds where she had lived all her life. Red geraniums adorned its drab and cracked brown stucco exterior. They filled not only the two window boxes but also the narrow flower beds flanking the entrance. Inside, there were splashes of bright colors everywhere. Most of the space in the front room was taken up by a modest hammock, frayed and mended many times, on one side, and a terrarium on the other, from which an exotic bluish-green lizard inspected the newcomer. From there a cramped hallway led to Liesl's bedroom and bathroom on the right and a comfortable little kitchen on the left where, when the weather was unpleasant, Liesl and Ulli sat down to talk or, from time to time, enjoyed a meal together that she cooked especially for him.

Ulli usually reciprocated with a little bouquet of wild flowers, and, when the linden tree was in bloom, fragrant linden blossoms for Liesl's tea. Sometimes he surprised her with sweet-scented elderberry blossoms which she loved to put in her pastries, and when the rose hips had turned bright red, he picked enough of them for Liesl to make jam that would last her throughout the year.

Together, they once saved a tiny blue tit apparently killed when hitting the cemetery office window in flight. Liesl and Ulli, hoping that it was just stunned, took turns holding it to their hearts and warming it until it recovered and flew away. Seeing their little bird soar into the air made them so happy they danced around the beautiful rowan tree that towered over the chapel, heavy with its orange-red berries. And afterwards, with just enough time before the cemetery closed for the night and Ulli had to leave, they watched the bats flying back and forth in the dusk.

In the winter, Liesl and Ulli, now and then, delighted in throwing a few snowballs at each other until, one day, a soft one accidentally went over the hedge. They heard a scream and then a woman loudly cursing the hoodlums who had nothing better to do than attack respectable citizens and threatening to report them to the authorities.

That strident and combative voice, they realized, belonged to none other than Olga, and Fluffy confirmed it by briefly coming around to sniff about, look at them, and wander off again. Since the shrubbery shielded them from Olga, she could not see them. And neither could she hear them because, as soon as they had identified their "victim," they stood motionless and remained completely silent, making a huge effort to suppress their giggles. Not knowing who they were, Olga who normally so loved confrontations, uncharacteristically beat a hasty retreat. Both Ulli and Liesl heaved a huge sigh of relief and parted with big grins on their faces.

In spite of the time that had passed since this little escapade, it was still vivid in Liesl's mind, and the memory of it made her laugh. With equal mirth she thought of the occasions when, over the years, she had good-naturedly teased and ended up irritating Olga at a place that she loved, an old antique-cum-jumble shop on a backstreet. Since Liesl had first discovered it, it had become her favorite destination, and she was so excited about it that she had to show it to Ulli. "Follow me, I have a surprise for you," she hinted one day and led him past the shop, then ran ahead, and waved him around the side into the yard where an old mirror was leaning against the building.

The mirror was dusty, and Liesl impatiently wiped it with the bottom of her pinafore. Ulli who had just caught up with her was wondering what the attraction was when he looked into the mirror for the first time. What he saw was a funny caricature of himself, constantly changing as he moved. "Why, this is a distorting mirror," he exclaimed. "How on earth did it get here?" Liesl, happy to see his interest and enthusiasm, told him that Bastl, the owner of the shop, had acquired it years ago when an amusement park was forced to close for lack of customers. And since he had been unable to sell it, he set it out in the yard so that anyone who wished could have fun with it.

Together, Ulli and Liesl walked toward the mirror and away from the mirror, hopped from side to side, made faces, and finally danced around, with their eyes fixed on their mirror images. It was hilarious. They watched themselves stretch and shrink, long and spindly, short and fat, upright or standing on their heads. One minute, they had necks like giraffes, the next, they had no necks at all.

Ulli thought he had never had so much fun in his entire life. They laughed until tears were running down their cheeks and, in their excitement, almost lost track of time.

Liesl had to return to work and, on the way, related how she had often invited others to join her in front of the mirror to have a good time. Most people, especially children and those who lived sad lives, happily jumped at the chance while others expressed their regrets for reasons of time constraints or physical inability. The only real kill-joy had turned out to be Olga. On the few occasions when Liesl saw her pass by Bastl's shop, she encouraged her to come and share her adventure although, knowing Olga's sour disposition, she did not really believe she would. And she didn't. With a look of contempt on her face, she stalked off in disgust, mumbling something like "disgraceful behavior which a lady would never stoop to." Without wasting time on this angry and arrogant spoilsport, Liesl, not fazed in the least, resumed her dance in front of the mirror, her peals of laughter following Olga down the street.

Unlike Olga who had turned up her nose at Liesl's choice of amusement, Ulli had loved it. In his silly mood, he spontaneously executed a number of cartwheels but so clumsily that Liesl was kept in stitches. It did not take her long to come back to earth, however. The idea of monkeying around and being useless for what seemed to her like hours made her feel guilty and uncomfortable. She chided herself for shirking her obligations and was anxious to get back to her chores. When asked by Ulli to go to the mirror again the next day, she declined, gently reminding him of the heavy responsibility she felt for keeping up the cemetery. That was where her heart was, and that was why she could not, in good conscience, drop all her duties whenever she felt like it.

Chastened, Ulli withdrew. Liesl had put her finger on the gulf that existed between them: She had a job that made her happy, and he was living on the streets. He understood perfectly but it hurt nevertheless. Maybe he had taken too much for granted, he reflected. They were pals, no more! So Ulli promised not to push Liesl to go anywhere with him in the future but to be patient and allow her to take the initiative. And Liesl had to admit it was a promise he faithfully kept.

CHAPTER

S uddenly running into Olga again after her winter-long absence took Liesl by surprise. She tried to keep a straight face but, with the images of the snowball flying toward Olga and Olga's waspish reaction to a little teasing at Bastl's mirror flashing through her mind, mischievously grinned from ear to ear. But Olga paid no attention, and nothing was said. Without wasting time, she headed straight for her family grave, briefly checked on it, and, satisfied that it was in order, left for the exit.

Olga's thoughts were not focused on the cemetery that day but on the beauty of the flowers that had sprung up everywhere, the invigorating sunshine in her face, and the melodious and soothing song of the birds. It was late spring, almost summer, and, unwilling to be confined within the cemetery walls, Olga was longing for the open countryside with its fields and meadows, its woodlands and sunny glades. After her miserable winter, she was now finally free, gloriously free to go anywhere she wished, without running the risk of bumping into Fabian.

To Olga's regret, the blazing-white hedgerows of blackthorn had already faded, its radiant blossoms gradually turning into sloes. Olga had also missed the golden cowslips in the pastures and most of the daisies. But the view was lovely. Tall grasses were quivering in the breeze, and, in the distance, brilliant-yellow fields of rapeseed reached up to bluish-green hills, reminding Olga of the wonderful scents of both rape flowers and the pines of the forest. Closer to home, the hawthorn trees lining the streets were in full bloom, shedding their white, pink, and red petals in clouds onto the sidewalks.

Spring fever took hold of Olga, and her enthusiasm for plants returned, not only for those in the garden, potentially beautiful enough to present to the flower show judges, but also for the poisonous ones on her balcony she would be able to use as insecticides. Most of her plants had died during the winter which left Olga no choice but to stock up on new ones. Still too cheap to buy them and not having learned her lesson, she again went out to pilfer any that were of interest to her. Fabian was behind bars after all; so who was to keep her from picking a flower or two here and there? I am not hurting anyone, she reasoned, and why should I ask for the plants when it's so much simpler and less time-consuming just to take them? It's not like I'm swiping all of them—just a few at a time. What's the harm in that?

So far, Olga had always been searching for plants within walking distance of her home. But now she was no longer satisfied with being limited to a specific area and seeing the same flowers over and over again. She was ready for something new. So when she spotted a used bicycle with a basket at the handlebars, advertised in the for-sale section of the local paper, she contacted the current owner and thoroughly and critically inspected his merchandise. She made sure the bicycle was sturdy and not fitted with gears and, trusting the seller's loose promise of a refund should anything go wrong, purchased it and proudly took off on it with Fluffy yapping in his basket. She steered it as recklessly as she walked in traffic, expecting everyone to get out of her way. But she did make it home safely and could not wait to show off her latest acquisition. No more horrid buses for her!

Olga's enthusiasm for her bicycle did not last, however. One day, on the way back from a farm, with some of its prettiest plants in her pocket and quite pleased with herself, she was looking forward to racing down her favorite slope. She so loved to cruise effortlessly that she was counting the seconds it would take her to reach it. As she was approaching the top of the hill that lay ahead of it, she pedaled furiously to increase her speed, and then let herself go. On the way down, Olga was in heaven. The trees were flitting by, and the breeze made her come alive. Olga felt like she was flying.

It was such a thrill until, toward the bottom of the hill, Olga caught sight of a flock of sheep slowly wandering across the road. She briefly glimpsed the old shepherd, shaking his fist at her and shouting a warning. Panicked, she braked with all her might and crashed. Fluffy was thrown from his basket, Olga landed on the pavement, and the shepherd was shaking his head, wondering how anybody, especially a fossil like Olga, could be so reckless.

Olga was lucky. Her bicycle had fallen over and skidded a few meters down the incline but seemed undamaged except for a dent and a few scratches. Fluffy, too, had emerged apparently unhurt and stood next to Olga, licking her face. As for Olga herself, all she had suffered were a few scrapes and bruises.

Typically for her, she made the most of her injuries. She moaned and groaned so pathetically that a few passers-by took pity on her and rushed to help her up. But she refused their assistance, claiming to be too severely hurt to be able to get back on her feet. She did not want good Samaritans coming to her aid, insisting instead on a ride to the hospital in an ambulance with its sirens blaring.

And Olga got her wish when the paramedics arrived. She became the center of attention which she thoroughly enjoyed, all the while whimpering and sniveling until she was lifted onto a stretcher and taken away, miffed that they did not see fit to turn on the sirens. That's the least they could have done, she muttered.

At the hospital she tried to keep up the charade but quickly snapped out of it when confronted with the humiliating diagnosis of nothing more than a number of minor abrasions. She was furious with the doctors, not only for exposing her deception but also for denying her the kind of attention she felt entitled to. The nurses did not fare any better. Olga was extremely rude to them and physically pushed them away during the examination. Upon being discharged, she made a spectacle of herself by repeatedly and loudly calling the entire staff a pack of idiots. Happy to finally see the last of this combative old cow, they sent her on her way without providing transportation, which enraged her even more. She was livid because, once again, she was forced to suffer the indignity of taking public transportation which she absolutely despised.

Sitting on the bus, she remembered both Fluffy and her bicycle and wondered what had happened to them and what she would do if they were lost. But when she got off at her stop, there they were: Fluffy, at the end of a leash held by Sylvia and wagging his tail, and her bicycle leaning against the fence. One of the good Samaritans had brought them back. Relieved to see Fluffy, Olga took him in her arms, but gave a vicious kick to her bicycle, hoping it would disappear. And it did. Olga left it out on purpose overnight, and to her deep satisfaction, it was gone the next morning. It had been stolen.

CHAPTER

With the arrival of balmy summer days, the neighbors' afternoon get-togethers in the common garden had resumed, and, as in the past, Olga punctually showed up but did not provide any food or drink herself. It was Hilde, Sylvia, Hans and Frieda as well as others living in the building who furnished coffee, cake, and pastries. But, unlike previously, Olga no longer came empty-handed. She picked a showy flower, usually from someone else's garden, put it in a vase, set it on the table for all to see, and then basked in the bliss of their admiration.

One afternoon, she arrived with a bit of news: According to an old man whose conversation with the butcher Olga had overheard, he himself and a friend had both received small packages with dead creatures inside, in his case apparently hideous beetles and, in his friend's, a number of crickets. Knowing Olga's nosiness, her love of gossip, and her habit of exaggeration, her neighbors were skeptical although, in this instance, Olga had been telling the truth.

Her story was confirmed the following day on the early morning broadcast: The public were made aware and warned of the ghastly parcels mentioned by Olga, circulating in the mail and containing not only beetles and crickets but dead snails, spiders, and grasshoppers as well. Recipients were encouraged to contact the police and leave their names, addresses, and phone numbers. As the subsequent investigation showed, they were all the very same people whose identification of Fabian as a con man had led to his prison sentence.

The person who had sent the packages, therefore, had to be connected to the case. The three suspects were Agnes, Simon, and Monika, and when the police visited the local post office where the packages had been mailed, it turned out that the individual responsible was Simon, Fabian's older brother. He was well-known there and had made no attempt to hide his identity. Strictly speaking, he perhaps had done nothing illegal, but the authorities, in concert with his father, thought it best to send him off to vocational school out of town.

With both Simon and Fabian out of the house, Agnes's life would have been empty had it not been for her daughter although Monika was away a good bit herself. As part of her rehabilitation and condition of her probation, she had been ordered to perform community service in addition to attending counseling sessions with Sister Maria. Agnes, well aware of her daughter's sentence, assumed she was faithfully fulfilling her legal obligations. But Monika was not, and neither did she have the slightest intention of ever doing so. Instead she was gadding about with her nefarious clique, invariably truant and up to no good.

Agnes was bored. With nothing to do, she drifted from day to day without meaning or purpose, fortifying herself with red wine until late into the night. She did watch the news, however, and her interest in politics was revived. Thinking about how she could help solve the problems affecting society, she had an epiphany: why not make speeches to disseminate her ideas for the betterment of mankind? Hyde Park, where people had their say on anything under the sun, would have been the perfect place for her to address an audience, but since, unfortunately, it was beyond her world, she had to be content with the pavilion in the park.

Agnes saw herself as a visionary, perhaps starting a new tradition. She would be the first of many speakers bringing excitement to the park which, due to her efforts, could eventually become a center of culture and innovative thinking. So, one day, after a great deal of preparation, she took the plunge. Her thin drab hair had been freshly washed and hung straight down to the shoulders of a turquoise, somewhat rumpled, linen shift. Her face was drawn with unease, and her complexion bare except for the faintest trace of tangerine lipstick. Although she was only in her middle to late fifties, her neglected skin and stern expression added years to her appearance. She looked like an aging hippie well past her prime.

Her looks notwithstanding, Agnes was a tough and resolute woman, confident that the public would be anxious to hear what she had to say. Wearing her most comfortable and well-worn leather sandals, she ostentatiously ascended the steps leading up to the pavilion which normally served as the venue for summer concerts but had been appropriated by Agnes as her podium. Looking around, she scanned the park for people her speech might attract. Then, after casting her trepidations aside and clearing her throat, she addressed her audience, initially almost non-existent but growing.

Ironically, her first topic was the correct upbringing of children. She spoke at length about how stuffy her parents had been, the numerous curfews they had tried to enforce, and their strictly imposing their will, especially on their daughter. They were "wrong, wrong, wrong," Agnes emphasized loudly. "Without freedom, I could not flourish or be my own person," she continued. "That is the reason why I have indulged my children's every whim, and I know that they are much happier today than my brother and I were, growing up. I am begging you, therefore, to be lenient with your children and allow them to think for themselves. Do not punish them or make them do things they do not wish to do," she pleaded with her listeners in closing.

The reaction to Agnes's speech was mixed. There was applause, and there were jeers. Those who knew how it felt to have rigid and cruel parents complimented Agnes on taking a stand. But their praise was drowned out by the titters and undisguised laughter of a small group of people who were familiar with Agnes's beliefs and the nature of her children. "You are a fine one to tell us how to discipline, or rather not discipline, our sons and daughters," one of them blurted out. "We all know how your children have turned out. All three nothing but hooligans. There goes your theory, you presumptuous cow. Society definitely doesn't need any more of your ilk, or crime would be rampant. If I were you, I would be ashamed. Get out of here and leave us alone," he concluded and stomped off.

Chastened and humiliated, Agnes was furious. How dare he challenge her and question her principles! She looked for the heckler in the crowd to give him the dirtiest look she could but, luckily for him, he was already gone. A few listeners were still standing around. They were embarrassed by the man's lack of civility and, although not necessarily in agreement with Agnes, gave her the benefit of the doubt. They believed that she meant well, at least. One or two even apologized, strengthening Agnes's resolve to carry on with her speeches.

Soon Agnes became an almost daily fixture of the park. Her words were contentious and sparked many discussions and arguments. But what was thought-provoking to some was merely entertainment to others, particularly when Agnes was not at her best but suffering from the effects of the red wine she had consumed the night before. She then occasionally stumbled, slurred her words, or lost her train of thought altogether, giving rise to laughter among those who found it amusing and regret among others who considered it tragic and felt sorry for her.

To make things worse, Agnes's appearances increasingly turned into a circus. Budding entrepreneurs set up shop, selling lemonade, cookies, chips, and other refreshments while the majority took it easy on the blankets and folding chairs they had brought from their homes. Even Monika showed up one day with her clique to see what her mother had been on about. Everyone was talking, not just Agnes. Children were running around and playing, and Agnes became merely a minor distraction in the turmoil.

CHAPTER

T he neighbors were not pleased. To them the park was a place
of peace, a refuge where troubled minds could come to heal
and find strength. It had always been a quiet oasis in the
bustling city, welcoming everyone to sit on its benches and listen to
the birds singing as long as they liked. But no longer. It had all been
spoiled by Agnes's never-ending speeches and the loudly bickering
and profit-minded proletarians in her wake. The neighbors' paradise
had been turned into a place of misery. Even in sunny weather they
had to close their windows to keep out the noise.

They decided to fight the disastrous intrusion on two fronts:
through the enforcement of ordinances, on the one hand, and a petition, on the other. It was Olga who brought their plight to the attention of city hall. When questioned about details, she undauntedly
stood her ground, providing all specifics relating to what she saw as
the wrongful occupation of her park. She was then assured that the
situation would be presented to the appropriate authorities for their
decision as soon as possible. Elated, she hurried home to give an
account of her progress.

Meanwhile, Sylvia, Hilde, Hans and Frieda tirelessly worked on
the petition. They collected signatures not only from everyone in the

building but east side neighbors as well. Zora and Adi, too, gathered signatures throughout the garden community and from all homes on the west side of the park. Agnes's house was the only one left out. It was Sylvia and Hilde who went to city hall together to submit the petition which was quite impressive as it contained signatures from all citizens living around the park, with the sole exception of Agnes's family.

Everyone anxiously awaited word from city hall. Three days later the answer came, and their efforts were rewarded. Those who had signed the petition as well as Agnes received a formal letter from the city attorney pointing out, firstly, that Agnes did not have, nor had she ever applied for, a permit to speak in the park, and even if she had requested one, it would have been denied; and, secondly, that public assemblies on city-owned property such as the park were illegal, and that this ban would be strictly enforced. A second official communication was delivered to Agnes alone. It was an order to cease and desist, putting her on notice that any infraction on her part would be prosecuted.

Agnes was beside herself with rage. She tore the letters to shreds, vowing revenge and screaming at the top of her lungs: "Who are these fascists to tell me what to do? I am not their puppet! I never even kowtowed to my parents! They can drop dead for all I care!" She then started taking out her frustration on her living room, ripping up the wallpaper until only pieces of it were left hanging, and cutting up a beautiful little oriental carpet into jagged strips of wool, piling them on the floor. She then pummeled the door with her fists and, in her frenzy, unwittingly struck Monika who was about to enter. What finally stopped her was the realization that she was no longer attacking an object but a human being. She looked up into her daughter's hurt and bewildered face and collapsed crying in her arms.

"What am I going to do," Agnes wailed. "They have stripped me of my purpose in life. My marriage has ended, two of my children have been taken, and you, Monika, are gone most of the time. The speeches were the only thing that have kept me going. And now I have nothing left. My entire existence is empty, and I no longer have the energy to create another meaningful future for myself. I might as well be dead."

"What are you talking about, Mother," asked Monika. "What has happened to you?" "I have been prohibited from making speeches in the park," explained Agnes. "Let me show you," she added and started looking for the two letters from the city when it hit her that she had already destroyed them. "Do not take this lying down," Monika advised her. "Let's sit down together and come up with the most spectacular protest these people have ever seen"—which is what they did.

A few days later, Monika and Agnes were ready to put their plan into action. After the sun had set and relative darkness had descended over the city, they retrieved a handcart from the shed and filled it with broken furniture and empty wine bottles from the garden. As they entered the park, they realized how brightly the moonlight was illuminating the grounds and, therefore, sought out the shadows cast by the trees to remain less conspicuous. They were nervous, and the crunching sound made by the wheels of the cart when they hit gravel only exacerbated their jumpiness. They slowly and laboriously moved toward the pavilion. Their cart was old and rickety and, under its load, creaked as if it were about to collapse.

When they had reached their destination, they carried their load up into the pavilion and dropped it along the outer periphery of the circular floor. They then kept going back and forth for more pieces of furniture and empty wine bottles until the entire pile had been transported from their garden to the park. Their final load consisted of Philipp's heavy scholarly tomes on geology that he believed safely stored at his former home, a can of gasoline, and a box of matches. Once everything they needed lay scattered around them, Agnes and Monika started to build a stack in the middle of the floor, beginning with Philipp's hefty books, topping them with pieces of broken furniture, but leaving the empty bottles aside.

Having assembled a rather sizable heap, they briefly took time out from their backbreaking toil. Agnes produced two bottles of red wine that she had hidden among the empty ones, opened them, and handed one of them to Monika. "This is quite an accomplishment," she said to her daughter. "Let's drink to our victory and celebrate!" Utterly pleased with themselves, they took a few gulps and then proceeded to dance around the stack, defiantly chanting "down with the fascists" and loudly announcing that the fun was about to begin.

"Be careful with the gasoline," Agnes admonished Monika. "Let's try the matches first." So they struck a number of them in an attempt to ignite the books. But to their disappointment, there was nothing but a momentary flicker which promptly went out again. The pages were too compressed to catch fire, and Agnes and Monika were too tired to pull out each heavy tome from under the pile and take it apart.

"Enough of the drudgery," they decided and, driven by impatience, poured gasoline into the stack and threw a burning match after it. Within seconds, it was ablaze. A sheet of flames rose from the pile, scorching both books and furniture until the entire stack exploded into a huge bonfire, spitting out fragments and sparks into the air. Agnes and Monika barely had time to step back and save themselves. Singed pieces of paper were floating around them, and the intense heat and smoke made it difficult for them to breathe.

The fire illuminated the park. Olga whose sleep had been fitful observed the flames licking the roof of the pavilion from her balcony. Alarmed, she hurriedly dressed, satisfied herself that Fluffy was still sound asleep, and ran downstairs to find out what was going on. Zora, too, had caught a glimpse of the blaze and sent Max to peck on Adi's door to wake him up. But most of the neighbors did not stir until Agnes seized one bottle after another and smashed them against the stone floor and steps of the pavilion, leaving a trail of shards and creating a dreadful and persistent din that disturbed the entire community. Countless drowsy faces began to appear at the windows and stare at the fire, eyes wide with curiosity.

Olga was the first to arrive, and the scene she encountered would trouble her for a long time to come. There were sputtering flames and clouds of smoke, and both Agnes and Monika were covered with soot. Intoxicated and still drinking, they stumbled around the fire, coughing, howling, and cursing the "fascists" for banning Agnes's speeches. A mass of debris littered the floor.

When Agnes spotted Olga, her features became distorted with hatred, and she immediately went on the attack. "You selfish and insufferable busybody," she screamed at Olga, "all you ever do is cause trouble. You have ruined my life. I am sick and tired of letting you get away with it. I am finally paying you back—with this," she added, picking up one of the few empty bottles left and hurling it at Olga. But she missed. Not only were her hands too jittery from all the alcohol in her blood but Olga had instinctively ducked to avoid the missile. Agnes's failure to hit her despised target added fuel to her fury. In her blind rage, she grabbed the can containing the leftover gasoline and poured it into the dwindling stack which, once again, instantly rose up into roaring flames.

A sudden anguished cry stopped Agnes in her tracks. Looking up, she became aware of the horrid sight of her daughter standing there with the front of her skirt on fire. In her frenzy Agnes had forgotten all about Monika who was now clutching her right leg in pain. Olga ran forward to help her, and so did Zora and Adi who were just reaching the pavilion. But Monika pushed them away and, pounding the flames with her hands to put them out, turned, jumped off the side of the pavilion, ran to the lake, and flung herself into the water. Adi was there to pull her out but Monika, stroppy and defiant as ever, slapped his hands away, making it clear to him that she could manage perfectly well on her own and neither needed nor wanted his help.

Dripping wet, Monika returned to the pavilion where she found her mother stooped over the smoldering ashes and broken glass, muttering gibberish and obscenities. She was in the process of propping her up when the police appeared on the scene. Seeing the officers took all resistance out of Monika but had the opposite effect on Agnes. She quickly came out of her stupor, lunging at one of the men and threatening to throttle him. She was taken into custody and, after Olga, Zora, Adi, and a few other bystanders had been questioned, transported off to jail. Monika whose burn injuries looked quite superficial was taken to the hospital for treatment.

Agnes spent the night in a cell where, exhausted from the evening's physical and emotional strain and heavy drinking, she immediately fell into a deep sleep. The following day she was charged with vandalism, disorderly conduct, public drunkenness, disturbing the peace, assault on a police officer, and resisting arrest. She would be financially responsible for a thorough clean-up of the pavilion and its surroundings. The entire structure would have to be returned to its previous pristine condition at her expense although, fortunately for her, both the ornamental columns and the roof were made of metal and had, therefore, sustained no serious permanent damage. And neither had the solid stone floor or steps. But she would have to pay not only restitution but a considerable fine as well.

But what should they do with Agnes personally, the authorities asked themselves. They saw her as a worn-out, half-crazy dipsomaniac who would not do well in confinement and might be more trouble than they were prepared to deal with. After consulting with Philipp, her estranged husband, they compromised. Agnes would be released into his custody. As for his daughter's offenses, Philipp asked for mercy which was granted, and Monika got off lightly once again. It was Philipp who ended up with the responsibility of keeping Agnes in line, a burden he did not want and was unwilling to assume. So, after collecting Agnes from lockup, he dropped her off at her house and went home to his.

CHAPTER

To Agnes it seemed the light, as dim as it had been, had gone out of her life. She felt empty, and her house was nothing but a hollow shell. Gone were the company of her children and the devotion of her husband. They all had their own lives to live and no time left for her. How had being a good wife, mother, and teacher really benefitted her, she asked herself, and came to the conclusion that it had been exceedingly strenuous and most boring and had done nothing for her at all. And neither had her lies, schemes, and deceptions led to any improvement in her circumstances. Her future looked dismal and she felt utterly forlorn. The walls were closing in on her, and the certainty that escape was the only answer increasingly took hold of her damaged mind.

To preserve the frail sanity she still possessed, Agnes had to get out. She took to wandering aimlessly through the park, not only in the daytime but also at night, often lying down and sleeping off her hangover on a bench until the sun rose again. Her home became no more than a temporary refuge, and the people she encountered in the park gradually began to fill the void in her life. Like a lost soul, she haunted them on their walks, hiding in the underbrush and periodically popping up here and there with such sadness and yearning in her eyes that most of them felt sorry for her and took the time to say a few pleasant words to cheer her up. Others completely ignored Agnes as, to them, she was nothing but a nuisance.

The cruelest perhaps was Olga. Entirely devoid of compassion, she would have loved to administer a thorough beating to Agnes although the fear of being observed kept her ferocity in check. Whenever their paths crossed, Olga turned up her nose and haughtily passed by Agnes, totally ignoring her or spitting at her and treating her like rubbish. Sylvia and Hilde, on the other hand, looked after her with kindness. Sylvia provided fragrant cakes and Hilde thermos bottles full of good strong coffee that they took to the park for Agnes to enjoy. And, once in a while, Frieda, too, contributed her famous aniseed biscuits or home-made soup as a special treat. Agnes received their gifts in silence but with a smile and, on rare occasions, recipro-cated her neighbors' generosity by offering them cookies of her own that she herself had baked in a lucid moment.

Zora and Adi saw to Agnes's welfare as well. On chilly nights when they happened to find her sleeping on a park bench, Adi brought a thick wool blanket to cover her up, and Zora sat down, held her hand, and softly sang a beautiful song to ease her tortured spirit. Agnes may have been dead to the world but somehow the warmth and sweet notes penetrated into her inner being and com-forted her, and, instead of wishing she had not survived the night, she was actually able to face the following day with a tiny bit of hope in her heart.

But it was getting colder and colder. Once again, the autumn winds were blowing, the leaves were falling, and the rains threatened to turn into snow. The realization that winter was fast approaching drove Agnes back into her own home on a more permanent basis. In spite of being despondent, she was not ready to freeze to death.

The first time Agnes entered her house after a lengthy absence, she was struck by the dreadful mess that confronted her. Everything downstairs was in shambles, much worse than when she had last taken note. The hallway was littered with leaves, pieces of paper, and other debris, and the toilet had not been flushed. The wallpaper and rugs she had torn and cut up in her rage over the city hall ruling were still on the living room floor. And a nasty smell emanating from the unwashed and moldy dishes piled up high in the kitchen sink assaulted her nostrils.

Agnes shivered. The heat was turned off, and she wondered if Monika was comfortable. She had to be on the second floor, that part of the house assigned solely to her and her brothers. Agnes called out to her but there was no answer. Apprehensive, she climbed the steps. Normally, she would have asked her children's permission to enter their private domain but there was no one to ask. So she haltingly proceeded and unlocked the battered door with her spare key, shielding her eyes when she passed Simon's and Fabian's rooms so she would not have to look at the almost total destruction of their contents.

When she reached Monika's room at the far end of the corridor, she noticed that the clothes line on which Monika's favorite outfits used to hang was pulled down and that the floor was strewn with nothing but dirty laundry. So Monika was gone. But where was she and how had she gotten there? It crossed Agnes's mind that she was probably with a boyfriend who must have picked her up. If not, she could have taken the bus or, heaven forbid, she might have used her mother's car, a frightening thought considering that she had no driver's license and had been in trouble for stealing her father's SUV in her early teens. In a panic, Agnes ran downstairs and outside to check the garage. It was empty, and Monika was in the wind.

Unable to deal with this latest blow, Agnes sank down to the ground and wept. This is how Sister Maria found her. She had stopped by for one of Monika's court-ordered counseling sessions, hopeful to finally catch her at home after having missed her countless times in the past. Agnes was a picture of abject misery. Sister Maria reached down to help her up and, as she led her back into the house, felt her shaking from cold and distress. How thin her arms had become, little more than skin and bones! Always tall and angular, she had lost so much weight during her months in the park that she now looked gaunt as a waif, and her threadbare clothes were hanging loosely from her body.

Sister Maria sat Agnes down on a kitchen chair and, once she had wiped the table and counters and washed some dishes, brewed a big mug of strong coffee and, with the oatmeal and little honey she found in the pantry, prepared a thick porridge and served it to Agnes. Agnes was ravenous. She savored every bite and every sip, and when she had finished her meal, her sense of well-being had been somewhat restored.

Now was the time to talk, not only about Monika but also about Agnes herself who took the initiative and opened her heart to Sister Maria. "I am warm and comfortable, and I am grateful," she told her. "Nothing should bother me now, and yet I feel so alone," she admitted bitterly. "Most of the people at the park were nice, and I always had someone to talk to but I don't know if I can face the winter all by myself, without a soul with whom to share my life."

"Monika has left me," she explained, "and I am so sorry you came here for nothing." "It wasn't for nothing," Sister Maria responded. "I was meant to take care of you and that is what I'm planning to do. I will send someone who will help you clean your house and make arrangements to have food delivered to you for a month. Do you think that will be enough time for you to get back on your feet?" "I will do my best," Agnes promised. "But will I see you once in a while?" "Of course," answered Sister Maria, "I will be happy to check on you although, for now, I have to get back to the church, and you need plenty of rest." She tucked Agnes into bed and handed her a warm water bottle to keep her cozy. "Sleep well, Agnes, and don't worry. I will see you tomorrow," she said. But Agnes's eyes were already closing, and Sister Maria softly shut the door behind her.

CHAPTER

29

While Sister Maria was hoping that the winter would give Agnes a chance for recovery, however modest it might turn out to be, everyone else in the neighborhood dreaded the cold and snow it was sure to bring. They regretted no longer being able to sit together in the garden and enjoy their coffee and cake on beautiful sunny afternoons. Olga was especially dispirited. Not only had she run out of beautiful flowers to show off at their gatherings, even if they were snatched from someone else's plot, but she had to admit to herself that for the moment her own efforts of creating the one blossom that would earn her a spot in the flower show had fallen painfully short. And so had her attempts of keeping nasty insects out of her home, in spite of her endless experiments with the supposedly toxic plants on her balcony. She knew there was nothing more she could do until spring.

Olga may have been frustrated but would never have conceded failure. If she could not achieve her goal, she reasoned, no one else could either. All she needed was more time. So she resigned herself to a temporary suspension of her botanical endeavors, vowing to take them up again as soon as she could. In the meantime, she would keep attending the meetings of the bird charity to remind its dignitaries that she was still a force to be reckoned with. And, of course, there were her daily walks with Fluffy to look forward to, especially the confrontations with the other dog owners against whom she would measure her wits. Olga was astute—there was no doubt about it—and usually had the last word. It was a game she delighted in playing, a game of banter, taunts, and occasional acrimony from which she would emerge triumphant most of the time.

As much as Olga enjoyed these encounters, even in the snow, she breathed a huge sigh of relief when, at last, the dark winter clouds lifted and the sun warmed the icy soil, and so did her neighbors. Their somber mood gave way to optimism and cheerfulness. On the surface, even Agnes seemed more positive than she had been for months. While confined to her house, she had slowly gained weight and apparently also some control over her personal demons. But she had felt shut in and snared like an insect glued to a fly-trap. Overwhelmed by the need to be unfettered and among people again, she ventured out to roam among the majestic trees of the park, free as a bird once more.

It was a beautiful spring. On market square, workers on their lunch breaks and tired shoppers alike rested on the benches surrounded by flowers and blooming shrubs. They had either brought their own snacks or picked up a bratwurst or two at the kiosk on the corner. They ate and chatted amicably, warming their faces in the sun. In the forest, the lizards, and sometimes a solitary adder, were dozing on warm and sunny rocks. The birds had finished building their nests, and their jubilant songs turned sadness into joy.

Life was peaceful until, on one of the first summer days, a scream shattered the serenity of the park. It came from a remote path close to Zora's cottage where a young jogger was making his rounds before going to work. Enjoying the fresh air and a colorful sunrise, he had suddenly found himself dazed on the ground, with a bloody knee and a cut on his hand. I suppose I was daydreaming, he thought. I should have had my eyes on the ground. But what could it have been that caused me to trip and fall, he wondered.

Looking around, he saw a woman resting on a strip of grass, her legs extending into the trail. He was about to apologize to her but realized when he got closer that his remorse would mean nothing to her at all. For she was dead, and it was the dreadful scene in front of him that had made him cry out. She could have been my mother, he was thinking. Shaken and sad, he felt even more distraught when he observed an old dachshund coming out of the bushes, with his leash trailing behind him, and, with a sorrowful yelp, lying down by his mistress.

There were no outward signs pointing to a cause of death except perhaps some vomited matter around her mouth. That's what it looked like to him. Other than that, she appeared untouched. He wished there were something he could do for her but knew it was too late. He had immediately called the emergency services and did not have to wait long to hear the sirens approaching. The site was cordoned off, pictures were taken, and the surroundings searched. The body was then examined and taken away in an ambulance, leaving a number of police officers to question not only the jogger but also some bystanders who were craning their necks.

Since there was no identification on the body, no one knew who the lady was although she had been seen walking her little dog in the park at least twice a day, and everyone agreed she had been quite friendly and had a nice word to say to everyone. But no one knew her name. Out of consideration and compassion for her next of kin, the evening papers refrained from showing a picture of the deceased. But they did carry an appeal to anyone to come forward who might recognize her and her pet by the following description: "Female, in her sixties, approximately five feet tall, gray curly hair, brown eyes, weighing about one hundred and fifty pounds, wearing a dark green skirt and navy top, and accompanied by her dachshund."

Soon the telephone at the police station was ringing off the hook. There were calls from meddlers who may, or may not, have spotted her once or twice, acquaintances, shopkeepers, her employer, and finally her family. Those that counted identified her as Bertha Schuster, age sixty-four, mother of one and grandmother of two, with whom she lived in an old and narrow two-story sandstone house on a cobbled street, south of the community garden. Frau Schuster was a widow who still worked as a cleaning lady to help out with expenses at home and spoil the little ones with a toy or special treat once in a while. She loved her family and Woofi, her dog, and would have given her last penny to anyone who needed it.

Bertha had been generally respected and well liked, and when, after the post-mortem, the toxicology report came back, showing that she had been poisoned with ricin, the police were stunned. For poisonings by ricin were extremely rare, except perhaps in cases of international political intrigue. So as not to jeopardize the investigation, the officials in charge decided to keep the specific nature of the poison strictly confidential. The public might not have known what ricin was anyway although everyone was familiar with its source, the showy castor-oil plants used as centerpieces in city flower beds and found in many gardens in the area. They had been told in school that their speckled seeds were poisonous and should never be ingested. There was no doubt, therefore, that Bertha knew it, too, and would never have put a single castor bean in her mouth.

When the realization struck that Bertha had been murdered, her family and friends were in utter disbelief. Who could have done such a terrible thing, they asked themselves. She had been a sweet and kind person who would never have hurt other people's feelings or harmed them in any way. Who could have been so angry with her as to want to kill her? It was inconceivable.

CHAPTER

The case was assigned to Inspector Michael Stein who, in his capacity as lead detective, began his investigation by visiting Bertha's family. When he rang the bell, the door was opened by a little boy whose eyes were red from crying. His older sister who was still weeping, pulled him into the scrupulously clean living room where their parents sat, obviously in shock and pain over the loss of their grandmother.

A respectable middle-class couple, the father earned his living as a carpenter and his wife worked as a secretary. They were clearly a loving family, each of whom was unstintingly cherished. On the little side table there was proof of it: photographs of all three generations in beautiful silver frames, most likely the most expensive items in the home. Next to her dog Woofi, Bertha's smiling face looked out at the inspector, and he could tell just how happy and decent she had been in life.

"There was definitely nothing sinister there," Inspector Stein later assured his colleagues. "On the contrary," he continued. "I was genuinely touched by the atmosphere of caring and good will that pervaded Frau Schuster's modest home and am really sorry that it's now tragically tinged with such sadness. I wish my own household were as peaceful. No, the culpability lies elsewhere. I am convinced of it."

Hoping to gain more insight, Inspector Stein set out the next morning to visit Frau Schmidt, Bertha's employer. Like Bertha, she lived in the old part of town where she had occupied the same flat for decades. She was eighty-nine years old, slight and fragile. When questioned, Frau Schmidt stated that the day before, the day Bertha died, had been the first time ever that she had not shown up for work. Frau Schmidt, therefore, had had no idea what had happened to her until she received a call from Bertha's daughter-in-law late in the evening.

Frau Schmidt, too, was heavy-hearted and kept asking: "Why would someone do this to her? She certainly would never have offended or provoked anyone. She was the nicest person you could imagine. She was more like a companion to me than an employee. Not only did she keep my home spotless but we also had the most enjoyable talks which I will sorely miss. She often stayed late to help me with something that was not her responsibility but just to do me a favor for which she refused to be paid. She did it out of the goodness of her heart, and now I'm all alone and don't know what to do."

Inspector Stein sincerely commiserated with Frau Schmidt. Although he had never met Bertha, he was beginning to like and respect her and was determined more than ever to find her killer. Like her family, her employer was obviously innocent. Without suspects or leads, the inspector was completely in the dark but hopeful nevertheless that the shopkeepers whose customer Bertha had been for years might be able to shed some light on her acquaintances or anyone else who seemed shady to them. He would question them next.

With a picture of Bertha in his hand, Inspector Stein interviewed the closest baker, butcher, and produce vendors. They all agreed that Frau Schuster had been extremely likable and always cheerful, rain or shine. They looked forward to seeing her whenever she stopped by after work to get her supplies. She was friendly and easy-going and always paid her bills. Unlike some, she was never pushy but stood patiently in line until it was her turn to be served. They wished all their customers were as nice as she was and expressed their profound regret over her frightful end.

The only places where Bertha was unknown were the cafés, most likely because they were relatively expensive, and Bertha had not been one to indulge in luxuries. She had saved all her money for necessities and her family, and it occurred to the inspector that she had not had a single selfish bone in her body. But where did that leave him? There was no animosity anywhere, no hatred, no malice, no jealousy, no bad blood, and, as far as he knew, no one had anything to gain by her death. He considered another appeal to the public but, doubtful that it would reveal anything new, ultimately decided against it.

Meanwhile, Bertha's remains had been released to her family for burial. The funeral was duly announced in the paper and took place two days later. The service was held at the Church of Our Dear Lady. Besides Bertha's loved ones, the mourners included Sister Maria, Frau Schmidt, and the shopkeepers, as well as many others who had known Bertha only slightly but were curious, sympathetic, or fond of her, among them Zora, Adi, Sylvia, and Hilde. Inspector Stein attended to show his respect and, at the same time, be on the lookout for anything that might help his case. But he was disappointed. There was nothing amiss or untoward.

The eulogy was delivered by Bertha's son with a humorous interlude by her granddaughter who recalled her absolute dread of spiders, putting a smile on everyone's face. "Grandma," she said, "refused to go into the basement because of the black spiders crawling around. They made her shudder. But she did love Woofi and all the birds," she added with a giggle.

It was a moving send-off, and Bertha was subsequently taken to the cemetery behind the church where an open grave next to her husband's was waiting to receive her body. When it was lowered, a blackbird followed it down, settled on the casket and sang its song until it was disturbed by a falling flower and flew off over the sea of beautiful bouquets and wreaths left in appreciation of how much Bertha had meant to her fellow human beings.

Although Bertha's fate had sparked quite of bit of discussion and speculation, the additional pieces of information that trickled in failed to further the case. Neither Sylvia nor Hilde could think of a potential explanation, and Zora and Adi were as baffled as Hans and Frieda. Even Olga, usually aware of every rumor circulating in the area, had no idea. She had recognized Bertha from her picture in the paper and remembered a little spat she had had with her over their dogs a few days earlier. "It was not heated," she reassured her neighbors. "Besides, who does not get carried away when it comes to their pets? If that's a reason for getting killed, we would all be murdered," she concluded.

Inspector Stein was just as much at a loss as they were. He sat at his desk, staring into space and trying to come up with a new angle. What had he missed? Maybe he wasn't as thorough as he could have been. In his mind, he carefully scrutinized his investigation but could not find fault with it. The crime did not make sense to him at all although it was bound to have made sense to the perpetrator. Who was he, and how could he find him? He knew people wanted answers and blamed himself for not having any.

His self-confidence was shaken, and he thought about his parents who had invested so much love and trust in him and whom he had always attempted to please while they were alive. What would they think of him now? They had welcomed him, their only child, with open arms, relatively late in life. His unexpected arrival must have upset the routine they had firmly established for at least two decades but, instead of complaining, they were overjoyed and felt blessed to finally have a beautiful little boy. The household Michael grew up in was caring and harmonious and full of kindness, laughter, and delight. He was cherished by his parents who did everything in their power to ensure his well-being. They also conveyed to him a strong sense of right and wrong and taught him to empathize with the frail and disadvantaged. No loud or unpleasant words were ever spoken.

Michael thrived. From the time he was a toddler, he followed his father around and tried to make himself useful in the old-fashioned, cramped shoe repair shop his family owned at the top of a hill in one of the suburbs. Michael loved the smell of leather, and it was in the cobbler shop that he observed his father dealing with his customers.

From a humble background himself, Herr Stein was well aware of how painful it could be to be poor. Invariably fair and honest, he never overcharged anyone and was known to apply a patch, or replace a sole, free of charge for those who could not afford to pay, especially the homeless who needed their shoes the most. For them he had a soft spot in his heart and, when their footwear was totally worn out and beyond repair, he provided them with shoes or boots customers had left behind at his shop or sometimes even a brand-new pair he had bought for them himself.

The one event Michael looked forward to most when he was a child was the soapbox derby held annually on the same hill where the cobbler shop was located. For an entire year, his father and he prepared for it, trying to come up with the perfect soapbox that would take him to victory: sketching numerous designs, sawing wood, making frequent adjustments, putting the parts together, and finally taking a preliminary version of their vehicle for test runs down the hill. Further improvements followed until they were both satisfied with its speed, and only then did they paint it in bright colors, write Michael's name on it, and finally apply a shiny coat of lacquer. Even though Michael won the race only now and then, he was always extremely proud of his soapbox. And being able to work so closely with his father made him realize just how lucky he was.

As soon as Michael was old enough, he regularly shoveled the snow in front of the shop in the winter and spread sand and salt to keep people from slipping and falling on the ice. And he did the same for some of the neighbors who were too weak or too old to see to the safety of their sidewalks themselves.

Since Michael's secondary school did not have much to offer in the field of music, his mother who came from a musical family, encouraged him to consider learning how to play an instrument of his choice. He asked for an acoustic guitar because he loved the way it sounded, and she surprised him with a beautiful specimen at the breakfast table one morning. His eyes lit up when he saw it, and, from then on, he could be heard practicing the scales, and eventually his favorite songs, whenever he could spare the time.

When Michael turned eighteen, he attended driving school and made his father's favorite old Volkswagen bus his project for improvement. He sanded its rust spots, spruced up the original dull gray paint with a fresh turquoise coat, and decorated it with all sorts of colorful shoes and boots and the name of the cobbler shop in fanciful letters. Very pleased with the way his "hippie bus" had turned out, he used it to pick up and deliver footwear whenever needed, and on weekends enjoyed showing it off, taking not only his parents but also his friends for rides into the countryside.

When the time came for Michael to settle on a profession, he realized that continuing the family tradition was not for him. Hesitant and afraid to hurt his father's feelings, he very gently conveyed to him that he just could not see himself as a cobbler for the rest of his life. For the old couple, it was a stab in the heart, one they had dreaded but known they would ultimately have to face. It would mean the end of the shop that had provided their livelihood for so many years. Although aching inside, making their son feel guilty or standing in his way would never have entered their minds. All they wanted was for him to be happy.

They hugged him and assured him that they understood. "Don't worry about your mother and me," Herr Stein added. "We will be fine. You have to do what brings you joy and contentment. And do you know what that might be," he asked. "I think so," Michael replied. "I have been talking to one of our customers, a retired policeman, who has been telling me quite a bit about his experiences, and law enforcement does sound interesting to me. So that's what I would really like to go into unless you feel that I shouldn't."

It was a choice that Michael's parents could wholeheartedly approve of, and they were very proud of him when he successfully completed his study and training. Together they celebrated his first job in the police department with home-made elderberry champagne and a mouth-watering bienenstich, Michael's favorite cake.

Upon retirement Herr and Frau Stein sold their shop and, when they died years later, Michael moved into his own flat in the city where a housekeeper did his cooking and cleaning for him. A plump and robust individual, she was quite competent and, from time to time, spoiled him with his favorite meals. Although she had five children of her own, she sort of adopted him and did not think twice about advising, or now and then even nagging, him on matters of life.

She reminded him that it was high time for him to find a wife among the hundreds of nice girls just waiting for him to make a move. For him, it wasn't so easy. He simply had not had the opportunity to look for a soulmate. He was too busy. And putting an ad in the paper as his housekeeper had suggested would have embarrassed him no end and made him feel uneasy. He knew his housekeeper meant well but largely ignored her meddling, hoping that he would eventually find a partner on his own, if he was meant to be married at all.

All this was flashing through the inspector's mind as he contemplated his inability to solve Bertha's death. He felt like he was letting down his parents as well as himself. In spite of his past achievements, his professional life, just like his personal one, seemed to have come to a painful standstill. He could not see a way to proceed, and the case went cold, at least for a while.

C H A P T E R

32

As homicides in his town were almost unheard of, Inspector Stein went back to dealing with minor infractions. The community, too, settled down and almost forgot about the unfortunate Bertha Schuster until, about three weeks later, another body was found at the edge of a vacant lot by a boy chasing a ball. In this case, identifying the victim proved to be easy as he was known to the children who led the police to a relatively humble rooming house where he had been a tenant for many years. His name was Oskar Braun, thirty-seven years old, a bank teller by trade but fairly recently also recognized for his paintings.

Inspector Stein was, of course, notified immediately. He found the site already cordoned off and a number of his colleagues and a physician on the scene, waiting for his instructions. As in Bertha Schuster's case, there were no outward signs of violence. Could there be a connection? At this point, the inspector had to be careful not to jump to conclusions. There was no visible vomitus, and, for all he knew, Herr Braun could have died of a heart attack. But the inspector could not shake the uncomfortable feeling that there was more to it than a natural death and ordered a full toxicology screen as the body was loaded into the ambulance that had been standing by to take it away.

Inspector Stein had been anxiously pacing in his office when he received the result that confirmed his intuition: Herr Braun had indeed died of ricin poisoning. The autopsy also showed that he had suffered from frontotemporal dementia, an incurable brain disease, which would eventually have claimed his life but had not advanced to its fatal stage and, therefore, had not been responsible for his death.

It was clear that both Bertha and Oskar had succumbed to the evil machinations of the same killer. But what could they possibly have in common? That was the question uppermost in the inspector's mind although he could not come up with anything that would have established a tie between them. Bertha had a family, Oskar did not. They did not belong to the same generation. They lived in different districts and had entirely different employers, Frau Schmidt versus Prosperity Savings and Loan.

But if Bertha had done her banking with Prosperity, the inspector surmised, there might be a link, and, hoping to confirm it, he made some calls to Bertha's family as well as to Oskar's colleagues. Defeated, he put down the phone. Bertha had had no account with Prosperity, and there was no connection. So why did they both have to die of ricin poisoning? It was a puzzle he needed to solve.

To get a better picture of what Oskar had been like, Inspector Stein went to see Oskar's landlord, Herrn Schneider, who, with his wife and children, lived one floor below Oskar. Herr Schneider, too, had been wondering just how on earth such an inoffensive and harmless man as Oskar could have gotten himself murdered. They sat down together in the landlord's living room to discuss Oskar's life.

"I have known Oskar for a long time," said Herr Schneider. "He moved in about ten years ago, right after his divorce, and has never once missed paying his rent. He was a quiet man who kept to himself although, whenever he sensed that I needed help with house repairs or yard work, he was always ready to lend a hand."

"About two or three years ago, Oskar suddenly became immersed in art, without having shown any interest in it before. It was as if a different person had emerged. As soon as he left his job, the pragmatic and conservative banker turned into this eccentric artist who felt an irresistible compulsion to create, often to the detriment of his health. He no longer took time for regular meals and lost a great deal of weight. But his pictures, in the beginning maybe no more than scribbles, have turned into rather unique and beautiful paintings sometimes sought after even by museums."

Inspector Stein who had discussed Oskar's diagnosis of fronto-temporal dementia with the medical examiner knew that his over-whelming and unstoppable need to create was an early symptom of the disease, eventually to be overshadowed by a deterioration of the patient's mental health and ultimately a destruction of the brain resulting in death. Since Oscar's illness had not reached this critical phase, he was possibly not aware of it himself, and the killer almost certainly spared him a future of unimaginable suffering.

These were the thoughts going through the inspector's mind when Herr Schneider added: "There really isn't much else I can tell you. Oskar had no children, and I have never met his ex-wife. According to Oskar, they parted amicably, and she is now remar-ried. His parents are deceased but I believe he does have a sister who studied abroad and never came back. His only real family is Belle, his German shepherd, whom I have been taking care of since his death. I'll show you where she spends most of her time. Follow me," he suggested, and together they went upstairs where Belle was sitting on the rug in front of Oskar's door, waiting for him to come home.

Herr Schneider unlocked the door to allow the inspector to view Oskar's flat and examine it, if necessary. His first glance into the hallway revealed hundreds of drawings of faces looking at him with huge eyes. They were pinned to the walls and led him to Oscar's study which had been converted into a studio full of canvases, sketch pads, an easel, oils and acrylics, countless pencils and pens, and pic-tures in various stages of completion.

Oskar must have spent all his discretionary funds on art sup-plies, thought Inspector Stein. In his imagination, he could see Oskar sitting at his desk or in front of his easel, diligently and passionately striving to express his deepest feelings in a colorful and meaningful way. He had to admire his dedication and tenacity and heavy-heartedly reflected on such a valuable and productive life having been violently and undeservedly cut short by a cruel murderer. The knowledge that he had also saved Oskar from a dreadful end, the inspector would keep to himself.

The rest of the flat was unremarkable. It was sparsely furnished, clean and dusted, and the dishes washed and piled up in the sink to dry. Oskar's shirts and underwear lay neatly folded in the chest of drawers, and two jackets, a suit, and a coat were hanging in the wardrobe. His nightstand contained nothing but a watch and a stack of letters from his sister. Oskar had obviously been an orderly man who had not been fond of knick-knacks. Other than his paintings, the only decorative items in his flat were a photograph of his pet and himself and a colorful metal container that used to hold lebkuchen long since eaten. There was nothing out of the ordinary.

Inspector Stein attempted to complete his picture of Oskar by getting in touch with his ex-wife as well as his boss and co-workers at the bank but, after questioning each one of them, remained just as baffled as he had been in the Bertha Schuster case. No one appeared to have harbored any resentment against the dead man. He had been unobtrusive, mild, and inconspicuous and yet had somehow made an enemy. At work he had been dependable, likable, and polite. So why would anyone want to poison him? What could the killer's motive have been? Nothing stood out that could remotely explain this crime, and Inspector Stein was at his wits' end once again.

CHAPTER

Weeks went by. Oskar had been buried, and the public interest in his murder had died down. Neither his picture in the paper nor an appeal for information on the part of the police had resulted in more than in few calls, none of them productive. The neighbors did not recognize him and knew nothing about him—all but Olga who was plagued by a gnawing and uneasy feeling of déjà vu. Was he the man she had had a confrontation with in the park, she asked herself. He did look a little bit like the photograph in the paper, and he did have a dog, a big German shepherd that wouldn't leave Fluffy alone. But, even if he was this Herr Braun, she thought, there could not possibly be a link between our argument and his death, and I would not want anyone to suspect that there might be, which prompted her to keep mum about her encounter.

The investigation had hit a wall when the third victim of ricin poisoning was discovered: twenty-three year-old Lilly Mueller, a hairdresser at the Metropol Salon. It was her boyfriend Ralf who had found her dead in bed, with her white miniature poodle howling by her side. It was immediately obvious to Inspector Stein that she had had absolutely nothing in common with either Bertha or Oskar and could not have been more different from either of them. Not only was she one generation removed from Oskar and two from Bertha but her appearance and lifestyle were anything but conservative. Her coal-black hair stood up in spikes. Big metal circles dangled from her ear lobes, and her right eyebrow was punctured by a ring. Her bright-red lipstick shone through the vomit on the lower half of her face, and a piece of chocolate had dropped from her hand. Lilly was fully dressed and, like the others, devoid of any signs of outward injury.

Even before the test results were in, Inspector Stein had been convinced that whoever was responsible for the deaths of Bertha and Oskar had also killed Lilly, in the same gruesome way, and he vowed that he would show no mercy to the perpetrator once he or she was identified. Man or woman, the murderer was a despicable coward, waiting and watching with stony and ice-cold indifference from a distance while the poison was invading, and slowly taking its painful and deadly path through, the victims' bodies.

Ralf as well as Lilly's fellow beauticians described Lilly as a lovable but tough cookie. A little flighty, she was late for work when she had better things to do and did not always meet her financial obligations. Her flat was somewhat of a mess, which was not unusual considering her age. Dust motes were floating in the sunshine, dirty clothes were piled up in a corner, and fast-food containers and paper napkins were strewn all over the table and kitchen counters. Lilly had clearly been a typical modern girl in her early twenties, no different from a thousand others.

Could Lilly's personal relationships perhaps shed light on her becoming a victim, the inspector asked himself. Her boyfriend was no prize. But he was harmless, completely under her thumb, and too unsophisticated and weak to even contemplate such a violent crime. It would have been totally out of character. Lilly had had no close girlfriends and, like many young people, was estranged from her parents. At work, apart from antagonizing a few clients whose hair she had ruined, she apparently had made no enemies. Did that mean she had been targeted at random? Inspector Stein did not think so.

But the answer eluded him. There was nothing he could sink his teeth into and nothing that grabbed his attention. He began to seriously question his abilities. It seemed he had gone over the reports hundreds of times, and yet he was still groping in the dark. His staff, too, had been busy interviewing anyone who might have useful information and collecting more and more materials for him to sort through, so far unsuccessfully. His solving the crime became even more imperative and pressing now that there was no longer any doubt that the perpetrator was a serial killer who had to be stopped as soon as possible.

The victims all lived and worked in different parts of town. So where and how was the poison administered? Depending on how much of it each victim had absorbed, it could have taken any number of hours to inflict harm and kill. Was there perhaps a locale where their days intersected? To find out, the inspector realized he needed to plot the routes taken by Bertha, Oskar, and Lilly, not just during their working hours but before and after as well. It would involve much additional questioning and would certainly be time-consuming but might finally point him in the right direction.

This was the status of the investigation when Hilde, Sylvia, Olga, Hans and Frieda, and a few acquaintances met for their regular afternoon coffee and cake in the garden they shared. Since the murders had been conspicuously publicized and extensively debated on the front page of the paper every morning, it was not surprising that they were loudly and animatedly discussed by the neighbors as well. Some argued for a madman on the loose in their midst while others pointed to the disgraceful incompetence of the police.

Only Olga was strangely silent. "You are so quiet today, Olga. Aren't you feeling well, or is something the matter with Fluffy," Sylvia asked, concerned. Olga decided to ignore her. Images of her run-in in the park with a young lady who markedly resembled the photo of Lilly and her little white poodle had deeply rattled and unsettled her composure. The circumstances were too odd and too ominous for her liking, and Olga was afraid that telling her neighbors about her arguments with all three of the victims might cast a shadow on her "lily-white" reputation and sow doubt and suspicion in their minds.

So, once again, she remained tight-lipped, got up suddenly, pleaded a headache, and abruptly made her exit. "I wonder what that was about," reflected Hilde. "But then we all know Olga. It must be one of her moods," she concluded. The others just shrugged, dismissing Olga's lack of courtesy as one of her typical foibles.

Meanwhile, the police had been hard at work, tracking the movements of the victims throughout the days preceding their deaths and finally establishing two possible connections: The paths of at least two of the victims, maybe even all three, had crossed at Bastl's shop, and all of them had been in the park where they had walked their dogs. As he looked at these findings, it dawned on Inspector Stein that his suspect pool had suddenly grown enormously and that it would be a monumental task to sort it out, but at least he finally had something concrete to work on. For the first time since Bertha's murder, he actually smiled. "Wherever you are hiding, we will catch up with you," he promised. "It's only a matter of time."

But the realization that these links represented only the first step in solving the crimes soon dampened his spirits. There was much more to be done. He still had to determine a motive that would tie the cases together and, most importantly, catch the culprit before anyone else came to harm.

As long as he did not know how or why the killer had chosen his prey, all Inspector Stein could do at this point was issue an urgent warning to the public to exercise extreme caution and, under no circumstances, accept any kind of food or drink from anyone while at Bastl's shop or in the park. To get the word out, he would hold a news conference which would give him a chance not only to alert the community to potential danger but also to explain what the police had been doing, and why it had taken him so long to finally discover a tentative connection among the victims. By being open with his audience—except for identifying the poison—he was hoping to appease, somewhat at least, those who had written scathing letters to the editor, lambasting him and his colleagues. More than anything, he wanted to be recognized as a fellow human being who was there for them and would do his best to justify their trust.

Much to his relief, the public responded favorably. They looked at the inspector on the podium and found him likable. What they saw was a decent and sincere man in his forties, conservatively dressed, tall, with closely cropped blond hair. His face was kind, his voice was soft, and his eyes were thoughtful. They understood that he had their welfare at heart and would work very hard to solve the crimes. Thanks to his practical advice, they would now turn down any food or drink offered to them at Bastl's or in the park, or avoid both shop and park entirely until the danger had been eliminated. Everyone was satisfied, and Inspector Stein had gained valuable time to further pursue his inquiries.

CHAPTER

t Bastl's, much had changed in the years since Liesl had first taken Ulli to see the mirror. True to his commitment to her, he had not suggested another visit, which Liesl sincerely appreciated. By making it clear to him how much her job meant to her so long ago, she had not intended to hurt his feelings, much less deprive him of her company which he so desperately needed in his loneliness. Touched by his putting her needs above his own, she had often toiled from dawn to dusk to be able to justify an occasional hour's break to have a little fun with Ulli in front of the mirror. On one of these visits, he had eventually met Bastl, the owner of the jumble shop.

Bastl was an elderly man who had been eking out a meager living, selling second-hand merchandise. The shop had been his brother's dream. Finding an affordable building in the middle of town had not been easy. But Alois had found it and was so proud of it. It was big enough to hold all his treasures. But Alois lost his life in the war, and Bastl, without much of a chance to find a decent job during the turmoil of the late forties, thought he might as well try to make a go of it although it wasn't at all what he had imagined his life to be.

But he managed. It turned out to be a lonely, impoverished existence which severely challenged his innate optimism. And yet Bastl survived and persevered. In spite of all the hard times, he never entirely lost his good humor or gave up hope to someday create something beautiful, interesting, and, if he was lucky, profitable as well. When Liesl first came to his yard and clowned around in front of his mirror, he initially observed her from the window but then went out to meet her. She was funny and made him laugh. That was ages ago, and, since then, she had brought quite a bit of sunshine into his life.

When Liesl introduced Ulli to Bastl, they clicked immediately. They sat down together and told each other about their lives. And when, one day, Ulli showed Bastl a gaudy mask he had found while rambling through the park and, in jest, held it up to Liesl's face, Bastl had an idea: why not use the odds and ends in his shop to be really creative and make all sorts of masks for the annual carnival? To compete with so many conventional ones on store shelves every October and throughout the carnival season, they would have to be colorful, unique, and maybe even a little outrageous. Ideally, they should be bewitching enough to practically jump out at the customers.

Bastl decided to give it a try. He promptly got to work and fashioned a number of prototypes. Those that turned out to be too time-consuming to make or were too fragile for the rambunctious carnival dances had to be rejected from the start. The rest he showed to Liesl and Ulli to get their feedback. If they did not break into a big smile when they saw them, these, too, had to be eliminated. Bastl knew he had to come up with better and more exciting ones. It was a painstaking endeavor but he enjoyed exercising his creativity. It was so different from staring at his antiques and jumble all day and having only a few customers who might not buy anything at all. He used to feel so lonely, being stuck in his old shop with no one to talk to. And, suddenly, it had all changed for the better. Working on his masks made the hours go by so much faster, and he could not wait to see his friends' reaction to his creations when they came by in the evenings.

For a few weeks, Bastl worked on his own but it soon crossed his mind how much more fun and how much easier it would be to have a partner with whom he could exchange ideas then and there. He thought of Ulli who, through no fault of his own, was not only homeless but out of a job. Bastl liked him and had been immensely sorry to hear about his accident and his father's cruelty. So, one evening, Bastl asked Ulli if he could imagine working with him in his shop. Ulli did not need time to think. He was so elated at receiving such a kind offer that his face lit up with pleasure, and he accepted on the spot. He could not believe his luck. He finally would have something worthwhile to do with his time again.

Any suitable materials that Ulli might find while roaming through the countryside they would combine with those they already had in the shop and, by putting their heads together, they were confident they could come up with spellbinding masks that people would love to wear. In spite of Bastl's weeks of experience, they were facing a lengthy learning process. They bought paints and taught themselves to carve and make papier-mâché. They practiced and practiced and practiced, using bits and pieces of glass, metal objects, beads, feathers, and whatever else they came across. It was a period of trial and error.

They patiently learned their craft until, one day, there it was: a mask they loved! Looking at it, both were struck by the same idea: It belongs to no one but Liesl. So they put it in a gift bag and proudly presented it to her when she stopped by after work. Wondering what on earth it could be, Liesl pulled it out, and this is what she saw:

The papier-mâché mask of a little girl with big blue eyes and fine features whose hair was covered with a white gossamer kerchief that beautifully framed her face. The fabric it was made of had been delicately embroidered with multicolored threads, tiny beads, sequins, and small metal studs which shone in the light and reflected their radiance upon the child's cheeks, making her come alive.

It was the most exquisite mask Liesl had ever seen, and it perfectly fitted her face. She was so touched by her gift and so humbled by Bastl and Ulli's generosity that she was almost in tears. When she had recovered her composure, she gave both of them big hugs. Refusing to take off the mask, she briefly went outside to admire herself in the mirror but quickly returned to join Bastl and Ulli in a celebration of their accomplishment.

And there was to be a big surprise for Ulli, too. Bastl who, for quite some time, had been thinking how well he and Ulli were getting along, almost like father and son, invited Ulli to live in his spare room at the shop. Ulli was speechless. He was blessed again. "Are you serious," he asked Bastl. "Are you sure?" And, of course, Bastl was very sure. He was looking forward to sharing his home with the nicest young man he knew.

Ulli could not wait to move in. Not only did he now have a purpose in life but would no longer be homeless. Having a place to live and an income, he was thinking, might just make it possible for him not only to rescue his mother but eventually ask Liesl to marry him as well. He had been crazy about her for many years, and they had been such good friends that her returning his love would mean that his happiest dream had come true.

As soon as Ulli had made his home with Bastl, the first tasks they set themselves were to clean the shop, sort out the inventory, give away whatever was unneeded or unlikely to sell, set aside little things they could use for their project, wash the windows, and make room for the display of their masks. Ulli who, as ever, loved to feel the fresh air and hear the birds sing still went out at daybreak to roam a little and, if he was lucky, catch a glimpse of Liesl through the cemetery gates. Both he and Bastl were happy. They had finally found a real, enjoyable calling that might turn out to be profitable if they worked hard enough.

When Bastl and Ulli had created a second mask that they found really pleasing and up to their standards, they displayed it in the shop window where it did not last two days before it was sold. From that moment on, their business took off, and their reputation grew. Among their first customers were Hans and Frieda who bought animal, story book, and flower masks for their grandchildren and Sylvia who placed a special order for an angel mask to hang in her living room. And the orders kept coming in.

Bastl's and Ulli's masks became so sought after that they often had trouble keeping up with demand, and, in no time, they were swamped. They had accumulated such a backlog that they were desperate for help. But where could they find the people they needed? Ulli thought of an acquaintance among the homeless who might be suitable, a middle-aged man named Alex who was tired of embarrassing his family and wanted to start a new life if only he knew how. And Sister Maria whom Bastl had consulted suggested that they talk to Katti, a young woman in her congregation, whose husband had left her and who now was living in dire straits.

Both Alex and Katti happily accepted Bastl's offer of a job. They were eager to prove themselves although Alex had a much harder time than Katti. Katti, it turned out, had always been interested in arts and crafts, had good ideas for new masks, and, with training, learned to make them well although not nearly as brilliantly as Bastl and Ulli. Alex, on the other hand, proved to be more practical than artistic, and it was to him, therefore, that Bastl delegated the acquisition and preparation of the supplies they used.

Even after hiring the two novices, Bastl and Ulli were still behind in their work, which kept them actively looking for additional employees. Gradually and steadily their business expanded, and eventually their shop turned into a thriving little community. Bastl glowed with happiness. He who used to be heavy-hearted and lonely was now outgoing and gracious. He warmly welcomed all visitors and, to spread his joy, offered free workshops in mask-making and put on little productions for the children, with music usually provided by Ulli. Zora and Adi, too, were fascinated by the beauty of the masks and frequently came to volunteer. And Sister Maria, inspired by the Turkish puppets, suggested that they add leather to their mask-making materials, a suggestion they gratefully implemented.

CHAPTER

35

Inspector Stein was, of course, aware of the excellent reputation Bastl's shop enjoyed. He remembered seeing a picture of one of the owners' first creations in the local paper and admiring their amazing artistry. He had wanted to see the beautiful masks for himself ever since but somehow had never gotten around to it. And in the meantime, Bastl's had turned into a place of immense popularity where people came together for work, camaraderie, or to lend a hand among friends. To the inspector it sounded like a fun place that he was finally getting a chance to know, even if only in his official capacity to begin with. Once the murders were solved, however, he thought he might like to offer his services to Bastl as a volunteer, perhaps playing his guitar during a children's program on weekends.

But first things first, he admonished himself. The sheer number of people going in and out of Bastl's alone presented a huge problem that required full cooperation from his team. The photographs of the victims were shown to both owners and customers alike, and many interviews were conducted. They confirmed what the police's tracking of the victims' movements had already established:

According to Ulli, Bertha Schuster had participated in one of their workshops so she could teach mask-making to her grandchildren. She seemed very excited about it and was fine when she left. As for Lilly, there was no question at all. No one had been able to forget her bizarre appearance, and Katti had known her personally. They had been schoolmates, and Katti recalled Lilly coming in and asking for the craziest mask they could come up with for a party she planned to attend.

When it came to Oscar Braun's presence or absence, there was no consensus. Unlike Lilly, he had not stood out but looked like hundreds of other men. Some claimed he had been at Bastl's, others denied it. But Inspector Stein felt there was a good chance that he might have been, in view of his all-consuming passion for art.

But even if all three victims had visits to Bastl's in common, how could they have been poisoned there, the inspector asked himself. Bastl's did not offer food or drink because of potential damage to the artwork. Nor would anyone ever dream of bringing anything edible or potable onto the premises. All questioned emphatically stated that they had too much affection and respect for Bastl and Ulli to expose their masks or preliminary designs to crumbs or spills. And when asked whether they had perhaps seen anyone distributing anything to eat or drink outside Bastl's front door, they all shook their heads.

That took care of Bastl's. It, therefore, had to be the park where the poisoner lay in wait. But Inspector Stein realized that finding him there might be next to impossible. If the perpetrator had kept up with the news which was likely, he would know that people, warned off Bastl's as well as the park, would no longer be easily deceived, at least not where he felt most comfortable. He would have to do his evil deeds elsewhere or discontinue them altogether.

It must have been the latter option he chose as no additional poisonings or murders were subsequently reported. Everyone was beginning to feel safe again although the fact that the killer had not been caught had led to a general sense of unease and indignation that he might have gotten away with taking three innocent lives for which he still needed to pay.

Once again, the investigation had stalled, and Inspector Stein did not have the slightest idea of how to proceed. To bring about a break in the case, he had explored all the avenues available to him and arrived at a dead end nonetheless. He racked his brains in an effort to come up with a solution but the harder he tried, the more difficult it seemed until suddenly an unforeseen incident appeared to move him closer to his goal. This is what happened:

On his way to his office one morning, he came upon a stained and crumpled piece of paper that had been shoved under the heavy front door of the station. Puzzled, he picked it up and looked at the few lines someone had written in a hand so jittery or disguised that it was barely legible. The scribbled note immediately captured his full attention. "What's taking you so long, Mr. Policeman," it said. "Haven't you figured out by now that Bertha, Oskar, and Lilly all had a row with Olga Lindermann right before they were killed? If I were you, I would get busy checking her out." It was signed "a concerned citizen." There was no name, and, according to the lab, there were no fingerprints.

But the message did give Inspector Stein something to work on. He himself had never heard of Frau Lindermann but was determined to subject her and her life to intense scrutiny as soon as possible. Before seeing her in person, he decided to do some research on his own. Public records showed that she was eighty-four years old and had never been married. Since she had been retired for close to two decades, he knew that making discreet inquiries at her former place of employment would be a waste of time. Instead he sent out his staff to the park in mufti to walk their dogs and mingle with the regulars, chatting with them and adroitly shifting the conversation to the subject of Frau Lindermann. Thus, he was hoping, he would get an idea of what kind of person she was and what reputation she had among her acquaintances.

His plan worked better than he had anticipated. Everyone had an opinion of "her highness" and was by no means shy to express it—on the contrary. "That old cow thinks she owns the park," said one. "When my pet so much as looks at hers, she blows her top, yelling and screaming. Her dog is not like other animals but more like a spoiled baby in his ridiculous outfits. He can do no wrong. According to her, his poop 'fertilizes' the lawn. It never gets scooped up, and our little ones have to be careful not to step in it. It's a disgrace!"

"She's a battle-axe who looks down on everyone else and always has a sharp tongue," said another. "She slings mud at nice people and is contemptuous of everyone else's feelings. Aside from arguing, her favorite thing to do is spreading ugly rumors, with no regard to consequences," said a third. "She's the most selfish person I have ever come across. She is rude to everyone including the children whom she chases away when they approach Fluffy," said a fourth. "What can I say," added a fifth, "other than that she is cold, pushy, and righteous. Not having a mate, she is jealous of happy couples and definitely vindictive although she can be friendly and polite when it suits her or serves her purpose. Don't let her fool you!"

Inspector Stein considered this a very harsh judgment, perhaps too harsh for him who, like Sylvia, believed in the basic goodness of human beings. No one can be all bad, he thought, and Frau Lindermann, too, must have some redeeming qualities. They may be hidden under her abrasive exterior but surely they must exist. I can't condemn her on the basis of hearsay, he reflected and vowed to remain impartial and objective until all the facts of the case had been established. A largely negative image of Olga, however, had already formed in his mind.

It was time for him to inspect the lady for himself and draw his own conclusions. When he identified himself on the intercom located at the entrance to her building, he was promptly buzzed in and quickly went up to her flat. The door was already half-open, allowing him a brief initial view of Frau Lindermann. She was standing there, dressed in simple dark clothing, with a tense expression on her face. In a gesture pleading for silence, she was holding her right index finger vertically over her closed lips.

She then motioned the inspector inside and, as soon as the door was closed, scolded him for coming to her home. "How dare you show up here," she shouted. "What will the neighbors think? They all know what you look like from the paper. I have been a law-abiding citizen and have never had any dealings with the police." Incensed, she glared at him, practically stabbing him with the fierceness in her eyes.

"What do you want with me anyway," she continued. "Couldn't we have settled this over the phone? If you had asked me nicely, I might have come to the station although it certainly is not a favorite destination of mine. Just remember, I have my rights and, as you can see from the picture of our last bird society meeting on the wall behind you, I know the mayor and could easily make your job difficult for you."

At that moment, Fluffy, rudely awakened by Olga's loud rebuke, started to bark furiously and charge Inspector Stein. "See what you have done," Olga chided him. "You have upset him no end, and I do not appreciate it." She picked Fluffy up and consoled him with soothing words, all the while casting hostile and accusing glances at the inspector who still had had no chance to speak. He had seldom experienced such venom at a first encounter. *She really is a nasty customer,* he thought. *But she does love her pet which so far has been her only positive attribute.*

Fluffy's constant yapping and Olga's belligerent demeanor made the inspector rethink his original intention of talking to Olga privately and informally in her home without putting her through an official interrogation at the station. Allowing for her innocence, he had been willing to spare her the potential humiliation of being spotted in his company by any of her friends or acquaintances. Olga's attitude, however, had made this impossible. When the inspector was finally able to get through to her, he told her in no uncertain terms that he had changed his mind and that she needed to come to the station with him. "I was prepared to go easy on you," he said, "but you have left me no choice. I will give you five minutes to get ready."

Swearing under her breath and leaving Inspector Stein in the hallway, she ran into her bedroom to quickly comb through her mousy reddish-brown hair, put on some lipstick, grab a jacket, retrieve her high heels, and look at herself in the mirror, tucking and pulling at her clothing. When she was finally satisfied with her appearance, she picked up her purse and joined the inspector.

She closed and locked her door as quietly as she could and tiptoed down the steps, hoping and praying the inspector would remain silent. And he did. He understood the awkward position Olga was in and had no interest in embarrassing her in front of the neighbors. He was too considerate and sensitive to do that to anyone.

In spite of the trouble Olga had taken not to draw attention to herself or the inspector, they were not unobserved. Both Hilde and Sylvia had overheard some of the earlier commotion and were wondering who in the world could conceivably be the target of such anger on Olga's part. They had even considered coming to her aid yet thought it wiser not to get involved. But they kept listening with their doors ajar and, once the inspector and Olga had passed their floor, hurried to their windows just in time to see Olga getting into a police vehicle with the inspector whom they, of course, recognized immediately.

What does this mean, they wondered. It was a momentous development they could not keep to themselves. They hurried down to Hans and Frieda's flat to share with them the most interesting event that had happened in the building in ages. They all sat down to coffee and cake and began to speculate. Was Olga in police custody or perhaps just a witness? Could she have used one of the toxic plants she claimed to grow on her balcony to poison the three victims? They did not believe it. They knew Olga was callous and often mean-spirited but surely she would not go so far as to kill someone. Besides, she had left Fluffy in the flat which proved to them that she intended to be back in an hour or two and would not spend the night in police custody.

Sitting across from Inspector Stein in his office, Olga was a picture of defiance. She haughtily looked around the room and, her lips pursed in a grimace of distaste, made it unmistakably clear that being in such surroundings was below her dignity. She yawned audibly to demonstrate her scorn and then impatiently banged her keys on the desk. "Stop wasting time," she told the inspector who had been watching her conduct with interest. His initial impression had been confirmed: She was a nasty customer indeed.

But was she guilty of the murders? That's what he had to find out. "Before we get started, Frau Lindermann," he said to her, "I would like to advise you that you have every right to call your solicitor and have him present for this interview." "What would I need him for," was her reply. "I have not done anything and have better things to do than sit here much longer, so just get to the point. What exactly am I being accused of?"

"We are not accusing you of anything but simply following up on a tip we have received," the inspector explained. "It has been brought to our attention that you knew, and were involved in altercations with, all three people who lost their lives to poison." "If I have ever seen them, and I am not admitting that I have," Olga countered, "it might have been at the park where everybody walks their dogs; and pets and their owners do get into scrapes. It's only natural. But we don't kill each other."

"Frau Lindermann, were you ever engaged in a confrontation specifically with Frau Schuster, Herrn Braun, or Fräulein Mueller," asked the inspector, trying to pin Olga down. "Well," she answered, "I did tell my friends that I came across a woman who looked like Frau Schuster's picture in the paper and her old dachshund who kept poking Fluffy, my purebred Maltese terrier, with his nose. He didn't like it, and neither did I. So I told her to go away."

"The other two I did not mention to my friends because of what they might think of me. Imagine, if they had really been Herr Braun and Fräulein Mueller—and I can't deny that there was a certain resemblance between them and those people's pictures—they might have thought that an argument with me led to their deaths. How creepy is that? Anyway, there was a man with a mean German shepherd who bared his teeth at Fluffy and growled at him, and a young girl and her ridiculously shorn white poodle that kept yapping and would not leave us alone. Of course, I shooed them away. What would you have done? I am not allowing any person or pet to disturb Fluffy's or my peace," Olga insisted.

Inspector Stein was well aware that Frau Lindermann was downplaying the extent as well as the ferocity of her rows with the dog owners. He was also convinced that these were indeed his victims. Even their pets were identical. Could the woman in front of him have been provoked enough to kill them? He would have liked to question her about ricin but at this point was not ready to disclose the specific poison used in the murders. Even if asked about poisons in general, he was sure Frau Lindermann would promptly disavow any knowledge of any of them, which is why he would broach the subject with her neighbors instead.

Unfortunately, there was nothing he could hold her on, at least not for now. She was not a likable person by any means, and, guilty or not, he would have enjoyed putting her in a cell to give her a taste of humility. But he could not see her as the culprit. She obviously loved animals and most likely would not have been so cruel as to deprive them of food and shelter by killing their owners although a strong enough motive might have impelled her to do just that.

CHAPTER

alling on some of the tenants in Frau Lindermann's building was next on Inspector Stein's agenda. Sylvia was just leaving when he arrived. She, of course, recognized him at once and introduced herself as Sylvia Seidel. He, in turn, stated his name and title and asked her if she was acquainted with Frau Lindermann and perhaps had a few minutes to spare. Intrigued, Sylvia answered both questions in the affirmative, asked the inspector to come up to her flat, and suggested that she fetch Hilde to join them. "Hilde is a friend as well as a neighbor," she explained. "She has lived here longer than I have and is a more realistically oriented person than I am. She thinks my head is often in the clouds, and you may prefer her judgment over mine."

Pleased by Sylvia's perception and consideration, Inspector Stein assured her that he would be happy to hear what both of them had to say. Sylvia was gone only a minute to get her friend and, upon her return, introduced her as Hilde Vogel. "Is Olga in trouble," Hilde asked and, without waiting for a reply, went on: "She's a strange lady, a tough old dragon with a mean tongue who thoroughly enjoys making life as unpleasant as she can for everyone around her. She feels she is better than any of us, and what she says goes. Getting along with her is not easy, and to keep the peace, we, from time to time, have to walk on eggshells. That's her negative and most visible side."

"That's true. That's how most people see her," interjected Sylvia. "Personally, I feel sorry for her. Except for Fluffy, her dog whom she adores, she is all alone. She grew up ignored, playing second fiddle to a younger sibling, her parents' favorite. Not having a soul to lean on or talk to about her problems, she must have been starving for affection and recognition. No wonder she developed a hard shell to protect herself from the pain of feeling rejected and at times even ridiculed. She had to learn to stand up for herself, keep a stiff upper lip, and never show her true feelings."

"Her sister died, her fiancé left her, and there were no colleagues or friends she could relate to. In spite of the correct and righteous image she cultivates on the surface, perhaps in order to be seen as deserving of the approval she craves, I believe that deep down she is insecure. She is very sensitive to any kind of criticism or put-down, bristles at perceived affronts, and will pick fights that usually end with her having the last word. That's probably the only way she feels she can prove herself and sustain her pride."

"Don't get carried away," Hilde admonished her friend and then continued, laughing: "There you have it, inspector, our professional assessments of Olga, one probably too harsh and the other one too soft, with the real Olga somewhere in between." "You are delightful, ladies," responded Inspector Stein, "and I am grateful. But let's talk about a serious matter for a moment. Has Frau Lindermann ever mentioned using any kind of poison?" "Yes, she has," said Hilde, "but never on people, just on pesky insects. She's forever trying to get rid of them by making concoctions from the toxic plants she grows on her balcony, but I do not think she has been successful. Just the other day she complained that, regardless of how many brews she experimented with, the ants were still coming into her kitchen and the wasps were still crawling around on her cakes."

"Olga likes plants. She has even come to us, seeking our advice on how to take care of them although we weren't much help. She borrowed some books on the subject from the library and might have consulted Zora Niculai, our flower expert who lives on the other side of the park."

Inspector Stein made a note of Zora's name and address, thanked Sylvia and Hilde for a most pleasant interview, and then went down to question Hans and Frieda. "Olga can be a pain," they told him, "always criticizing someone or something. She is hard to please, and we call her 'her highness' because she treats us as lackeys. It riles us no end but we grin and bear it to keep the peace. That sums it up in a nutshell." "Other than Frau Seidel and Frau Vogel, is there anyone else in this building who regularly associates with Frau Lindermann," inquired the inspector. "Not really," replied Hans. "They are mostly younger people who come and go and wouldn't be interested in fraternizing with someone her age."

Having questioned all of Olga's immediate neighbors who could be of assistance to him, Inspector Stein made his way across the park to interview Zora. She was watering her flowers when he arrived, and, as soon as she found out who he was, welcomed him into her living room with a smile and offered him coffee and pastries which he gladly accepted. What a sweet lady, he thought, and quite exotic, too. Zora's face and dark eyes radiated kindness and made him feel happy to be in her company. Her colorful off-beat clothing fascinated him, and he admired the way many vivid hues came together in perfect harmony in her little house. That Zora was special, there was no doubt in his mind, and he was prepared to trust her judgment without reservations of any kind.

For the moment, he enjoyed just sitting there with her, looking at her, and wishing she were the godmother he had never had. Reluctantly he finally turned to her with the questions he had come to ask. "I understand," he said, "that Olga Lindermann might have requested your guidance on the cultivation of plants," which Zora confirmed with a nod. "Since that's the case," he continued, "did she ever bring up poisonous ones?" "Not in the beginning," responded Zora. "She just stood at my gate one day, mesmerized by my flowers which ultimately inspired her to take up botany as a hobby."

"Initially she only wanted to learn how to care for plants in general but slowly became more ambitious, aspiring to develop her own insecticides that would not harm Fluffy, her dog. So I assume she would be familiar with plants like geraniums that are toxic to some insects but not really to people or animals. Her ultimate goal is to create a blossom lovely enough to be entered in a flower show. So she's always looking for strikingly beautiful plants although she does not know how to encourage their growth and most likely never will."

"Two such flowers she discovered were extremely poisonous. The first one, a deadly nightshade, she came across in the woods, and the second one, a red angel's trumpet she tried to hide in her basket on her way back from the cemetery one day. To the best of my recollection, these two are the only deadly plants that I know personally Frau Lindermann is aware of."

"What is your general impression of her," asked the inspector. "Do you feel she might be capable of poisoning someone?" Before Zora could answer, they heard the rhythmic sound of big wings approaching and saw Max alighting on the window sill. With his head tilted to one side, he looked at the inspector and made him laugh. "That's Max, my pet crow," Zora explained. "He's the one who recovered my stolen coin a year or two ago." "I thought he might be. It's wasn't my case but I heard about it. What a smart bird," the inspector said, amazed.

Olga was to be forgotten a while longer for at that moment someone bounced up the steps and knocked on the door. It turned out to be Adi. Zora introduced him as her friend and neighbor Adi Pollock. The men shook hands, and Inspector Stein told Adi about the purpose of his visit. "I should have known that it would be about Olga, the bane of our existence," said Adi mischievously. "Seriously though, she's not that bad. She's the kind of person who thinks the sun rises and sets with her even if her morals aren't exactly white as snow. At least she doesn't live next-door, and we don't have to put up with her too often."

Zora agreed, merely adding that, in spite of appearances, she was fairly certain that Olga would not commit murder. Inspector Stein thanked her cordially, not only for the information she had provided but also for her warm hospitality. He had felt so content in her home that he was sorry to leave. "Could I come and see you again on my own time," he shyly asked." "Of course, please do," was Zora's reply. "I will be happy to welcome you and maybe I will sing you a song."

Inspector Stein walked away, smiling. His lightheartedness was not to last, however, for he suddenly remembered that he still needed to follow up on Frau Vogel's observation that Frau Lindermann might be growing toxic plants on her balcony. He was by no means looking forward to confronting her sour face again but might as well get it over with, the sooner, the better.

He caught up with her just as she was checking her mail at the building's entrance. "What do you want now," she demanded to know. "I would like to take a look at your balcony," answered the inspector, "if you don't mind." "I do mind," insisted Olga, "but I suppose there is nothing I can do to keep people like you from harassing me and invading my privacy." Turning her back to him, she started to go upstairs, and the inspector followed. He waited for her to unlock her door and walked in before she could shut it in his face.

What a contrast between Frau Niculai's welcoming smile and this woman's ungracious reception, he thought. It's like the difference between a serene sunny day and a destructive tornado. With Olga's suspicious eyes on him, he then went out onto the balcony where he found only marigolds, mint, and a few other herbs that might be irritating to insects. Regrettably there were no castor-oil plants at all. He had wanted Frau Lindermann to be guilty, and taking her into custody would have made his day but unfortunately was unwarranted for the time being. Frustrated, he let himself out.

CHAPTER

B ack at the station, Inspector Stein did his best to collect his thoughts and perceive some logic in the murders, the poison used, the victims, and the circumstances surrounding the killings. He read and reread the copious notes he and his team had taken and, regardless of how many times he went over them, he kept arriving at the same dead-end conclusion: He did have a suspect although a very unlikely one, a woman in her eighties with no criminal record, not even a minor infraction in her entire life. Olga Lindermann was a snob and had definitely stepped on many toes and alienated, snubbed, patronized, and offended countless people, but why would she suddenly use poison to get rid of them altogether? There was no evidence for that, and it did not make sense.

Inspector Stein was tired of plodding. What he needed was a flash of insight, a bright idea, a sudden revelation. But none came to him. His intuition had failed him miserably. References to the homicides had long been relegated to the inside pages of the paper, and Bertha, Oskar, and Lilly had largely been forgotten except by the inspector whom they haunted every day. He who had always prided himself on being able to think sensibly and logically had nearly lost hope of solving this case.

Fall was quickly approaching. The summer heat had subsided, and the park was turning into a colorful mosaic of greens, yellows, oranges, and reds. Some birds were still singing in the trees although many of them would soon be on their way to warmer climates, and most of the branches would be bare. Zora hurried into the woods to gather the last chanterelles she would find before the cold weather set in. They were her favorite edible mushrooms. The ones she really loved, however, were the poisonous fly agaric toadstools with their bright-red caps and luminous white spots. They made the greenish-brown undergrowth come alive, and Zora delighted in coming upon them during her walks through the brush.

Inspector Stein had his heart set on clearing up the poisonings before snow and ice covered the community and yet had no idea how to achieve his goal nor the confidence that he would. Unexpectedly, however, a glimmer of hope reenergized his investigation. Another anonymous note had arrived. Just like the first one, it had been pushed under the massive front door of the station. Written in the same nearly illegible hand on the same type of crumpled paper, it, too, was free of fingerprints. The unsigned message read: "Do I have to spell out every single step for the police to take? Are you all dense and blind? Have you checked out Olga Lindermann's garden plot? If not, it's high time you did."

Inspector Stein was so loath to deal with Olga again that he was tempted to pay no attention to the note at all. But he would not be doing his job if he ignored information received from the public, even if it was sometimes worthless, nonsensical, or obstructive. Before he could bring himself to face Olga in person, however, he wanted to make sure that this garden plot was real and not the product of someone's imagination. He called Sylvia who confirmed that Olga had indeed been given a flower bed in the shared garden for her own use. Could there be something to it, the inspector asked himself, his dread of having to confront Olga softened by cautious optimism.

Admitted into the building by Sylvia, he braced himself for a heated face-off with Olga, climbed the stairs, and rang her doorbell. It was answered by Fluffy's furious barking and Olga's sharp demand for him to identify himself. "You again," she shouted. "I have warned you. You keep bothering me, and your job will be on the line. Like it or not, this is absolutely the last time I am talking to you. I don't want to see you here ever again. Now what exactly is the purpose of your visit?"

"I would like you to show me your garden plot," answered the inspector. Olga asked why she should but received no reply. "Just a minute," she suddenly said, ran off, and came back with what looked like a fancy old walking stick, perhaps her grandfather's, and repeatedly banged it against the wall. "Insufferable young people," she growled. "The racket they make will drive anyone insane. But they don't care." Inspector Stein who had been totally unaware of any discernible noise coming from the adjacent flat, took this as one more indication of Olga's combativeness. It must be hell being her neighbor, he thought, and I wouldn't be surprised if she hit me next.

"Again, what was it you wanted," Olga demanded to know after putting away the cane, making Inspector Stein repeat his request that she take him to the small section of the grounds allocated to her. Resigned, she led him to a corner in the common garden where her flower bed was located. "That's it," she said and pointed to a relatively small untidy jumble of diverse plants, weeds, and dead stalks, surrounded by a haphazard border of calendula, a kind of sage, and forget-me-nots. The entire plot looked sad and neglected.

In the middle of it all was an eye-catching centerpiece, a healthy castor-oil plant sunk into the ground in what looked like the original pot, only the rim of which was still visible. With its red stems and large, lobed, dark purplish-green leaves, it looked quite beautiful. Only a few of the yellowish flowers remained, most of them replaced by spiny pods. Some of these had already split, and the mottled brownish seeds they had ejected lay scattered on the ground. This was the plant Inspector Stein had been looking for. Could it possibly be the source of the ricin used in the murders?

Totally indifferent to the inspector's scrutiny of her plot, Olga had been distracted by a rare butterfly on a neighboring shrub until his voice startled her and brought her back to reality. "Do you know the big plant in the middle," he asked. That's when Olga consciously looked at her flower bed for the first time that day and felt utterly perplexed. "Of course I know it," she stuttered. "It's a castor-oil plant. Everybody knows it. But how did it get here? Who could have planted it? I certainly did not and simply cannot comprehend what is happening to me and my life."

There was no mistaking the genuine bewilderment in Olga's eyes. Something inexplicable and alarming was taking place, something it was not in her power to control. Inspector Stein could not help feeling sorry for her as he saw her puzzlement turn into fear. At that moment she was no longer the dragon he disliked but an old lady he pitied. Olga had clearly been framed by the real perpetrator, and there was no doubt in his mind that she was innocent.

If not Olga, then who? Obviously no one was really fond of her but who hated her enough to go to such lengths to get her convicted of the murders and condemned to rot in prison for the rest of her life? Inspector Stein was certain that it was not one of the people he had already interviewed since all of them had been more than fair in their assessment of Olga's character. It had to be the same individual who had written the two notes, he concluded. At a complete loss as to how to identify him, he was stymied once more.

But he had not counted on Olga. Unable to sleep with indignation and outrage that someone had dared to invade her domain, she lay in bed, thinking about what she needed to do to restore her peace of mind. Having made a satisfactory decision, she finally dozed off shortly after midnight. At the break of dawn she was ready to carry out her plan. She got up and dressed quietly so as not to disturb Fluffy, grabbed a shovel and rake from the balcony, and let herself out.

She anxiously hurried downstairs and out the front door which she carefully left ajar as the loud bang with which it usually closed would have alerted her neighbors. What she needed to do, she would do in private. She crossed the garden to her own corner and started digging. The soil was still moist from the last rain which made it easy for her, and, in no time, she was able to lift out the alien plant, still in its pot.

She had intended to get rid of it by throwing it into the dumpster but, after taking a good look at it, became visibly excited and decided to leave it for Inspector Stein to see. At a quarter to eight she was already standing in front of the station, impatiently waiting for him to arrive. She was pacing back and forth, endlessly it seemed to her, although the inspector appeared only five minutes later, punctual for work as usual.

Quite surprised to find Olga on his doorstep, he bade her a pleasant good morning. What on earth could have brought her here, he wondered. Judging by her expression, it had to be a matter she deemed of the utmost importance. Her normal surliness had left her face, replaced by smugness and occasional flickers of triumph. She was so eager to tell him what she had discovered that she refused to sit down but insisted that he accompany her back to her plot immediately so she could show him the plant she had dug up, in its pot.

"At first it looked like a simple container," she announced, "because all we could see yesterday was the rim. When I had removed most of the dirt, however, I noticed that it was a distinctive melamine pot with a molded design of leaves and blossoms over most of its body and a smooth inch-wide edge around the top. I recognized it immediately. It was a pot I had seen in Agnes Berger's yard."

Inspector Stein followed Olga to her flower bed to inspect the pot for himself. He had to admit that it seemed rather unique and looked unlike anything he had seen at either of the two local garden centers. Frau Lindermann might have a point, he conceded, although he did not want to be too optimistic for fear that his hopes might be dashed again. He could not deny, however, that Olga's discovery had encouraged him considerably. He praised her for her perspicacity and shrewdness, thanked her profusely for the help she had provided, and promised to keep her up to date on the progress of the investigation, leaving her basking in gratification and pride. The plant and pot he took to the station where he would call his colleagues together to determine any further action that had to be taken.

CHAPTER

W hat did they know about the Berger family, was the first question they asked. "I have done a bit of research," replied the inspector, "and this is what I've found: The Bergers are not unknown to us—on the contrary. As for the head of the family, Philipp Berger, he does not concern us. He is a respected scientist and businessman who is separated from his wife Agnes but has remained a good and generous provider for her and the children. He has not shared a residence with them for quite some time and, other than giving them both financial and hands-on support, has practically nothing to do with them any longer. If you want my opinion, he is a lucky devil to have gotten away."

"As for the rest of them, they are a nasty bunch. First the three children, Simon, nineteen, Monika, eighteen, and Fabian, seventeen years old. Let's start with Fabian. He has been convicted of fraud and theft targeting the weak and ailing and is currently serving a prison sentence. Sister Maria, incidentally, has been very helpful to me by providing additional information. For those of you who are not familiar with her, she's a lay sister at the Church of Our Dear Lady and, as such, in certain instances bound by confidentiality. Without mentioning names or specific circumstances, therefore, she has indicated to me that Fabian was, no doubt, guilty of other serious offenses such as blackmail as well. But he is behind bars and could not have killed our victims."

"Unlike Fabian, Simon is not a hardened criminal but actually the most acceptable of the siblings. The only time he has come to our attention was when he mailed dead insects and other creatures to the witnesses who had identified, and testified against, his brother, resulting in Fabian's conviction. Simon was subsequently sent out of town by his father to give him the opportunity to start a new life and pursue a proper career. So he, too, is out of the picture."

"Monika is the most recalcitrant of all. She has probably been on the fringes of petty crime the longest. She is part of a clique or rather a teenage gang responsible for major acts of vandalism. They are totally amoral and always do as they please regardless of propriety or the law which mean absolutely nothing to them. According to Sister Maria who supervises her court-ordered community service and counseling sessions, Monika has not once bothered to show up for any of them."

"All three siblings have a record of truancy; Fabian and Monika more so than Simon. Monika has always been close to her mother which, unfortunately, has corrupted her even further. As you might remember, they egged each other on when they started the huge fire in the park, damaging the pavilion and breaking countless bottles in their drunken rage. As usual, it was not the culprits but Philipp, the father, who paid restitution and the fines they incurred."

"Since that incident Frau Berger has apparently taken to spending more and more time in the park where she has been seen wandering aimlessly, drinking, and spending entire nights on benches, except in the winter. On one occasion last fall when she returned home as she periodically did, especially when it got too cold for her outside, Sister Maria found her crying inconsolably in front of her house. She had just discovered that Monika had not only deserted her but taken her car as well, which Agnes considered the ultimate betrayal. To this day, Monika has not been seen or heard from again and can, therefore, also be eliminated as a suspect."

"That leaves only Agnes Berger, the mother. Apart from stealing a gold coin from a neighbor which was later recovered, she has committed only relatively minor violations such as vagrancy and appropriating and damaging public property, most of it in a state of intoxication."

"She does have a history with Frau Lindermann, however. I understand that their feud goes way back. To keep it brief, neither of them will suffer insults, and there is no respect for the other on either side. Frau Lindermann who is single has reportedly always begrudged Frau Berger her marital status and then made her a laughingstock when her husband left her. For years she has gloated over her children's delinquency and loudly advertised it to anyone who would listen. A busybody by nature, she would hang around the Bergers' property to snatch plants she liked or collect material for the rumors she enjoyed spreading. Many bitter quarrels ensued, and their relationship, already acrimonious, inevitably turned into open hostility, maybe even hatred."

"You might remember that it was Frau Lindermann who, by lodging a complaint against Frau Berger at city hall, became instrumental in putting an end to her speeches in the park. It was also Frau Lindermann who showed up at the fire, by her presence provoking an attack by Frau Berger who screamed at her and accused her of having ruined her life. She also threw a bottle at her which fortunately missed. Frau Lindermann, in turn, has been observed spitting at Frau Berger, not just once but multiple times. And, according to witnesses, all passers-by, Frau Lindermann did not confine her venom to spitting but on those occasions also vociferously hurled degrading epithets at her nemesis."

"That wraps it up as far as the Berger family goes," Inspector Stein concluded and, addressing his team, added: "Let's go search the Berger premises!" Finally a real prospect, he thought, something concrete to sink his teeth into. When they arrived at the Bergers' address, they found themselves in front of a large, modern, red-brick structure, with the built-in garage and entrance facing the street and a spacious fenced yard around the back and extending to the sides, a home anyone could be proud of, at least on the face of it.

At Inspector Stein's suggestion, they first entered the yard, and what they discovered was the opposite of what they would have expected to see behind a nice upper middle class home. It was littered with debris, and the few flowers and vegetables that remained were fighting a losing battle against the stifling overgrowth of weeds. Adjacent to the exterior steps leading down to the basement, there was an enormous pile of broken furniture under which someone had pushed countless wine bottles, perhaps in an unsuccessful attempt to hide them from view. They were still visible, however, some of them whole and others smashed to pieces.

It was a somber place of dereliction that the police officers were more than ready to leave until one of them spotted a stack of flower pots in a corner. He pulled it apart, and there it was, the exact twin of the one on Olga's plot. It was proof they were on the right track. They picked it up, secured it in their vehicle, and then approached the building itself.

The garage stood open. It was strewn with twigs and leaves blown in by the wind and obviously had not sheltered a car for quite some time. The front door was ajar although a spider had labored to close the crack with its web. They nudged it open and found themselves in a nightmare.

Wherever they looked, there was destruction. Incredulous, they took in the walls and ceilings smeared with food and graffiti, a few shreds of wallpaper hanging here and there. The lampshades were sliced, the light bulbs shattered. The books had been pulled off the shelves, and their ripped pages had joined the scraps of carpet and frayed rugs on the floors. The unwashed dishes in the sink had grown a moldy coating, the faucet was dripping, and the fetid smells emanating from the bathroom and kitchen made them wish they had brought their masks.

But there was one item that was still intact: It was a doll looking down from its perch on top of the battered desk. Someone had clearly made it by hand, painstakingly recreating reality in all its details. Inspector Stein immediately recognized it as an effigy of Olga. Three pins with differently colored heads protruded from its chest which, he theorized, might be symbolic of the three murders that had been intended to land Frau Lindermann in prison.

An eerie silence pervaded the house. Deeply troubled, the officers proceeded upstairs, looking for signs of life. But there, too, all they found was devastation. The doors carried nameplates which identified the entire floor as the children's realm. There they must have amused themselves, wreaking havoc to their hearts' content and leaving scars behind that no one had troubled to mend since their departure.

Appalled, Inspector Stein and his team turned their backs on the ruins and descended the interior stairs down to the basement. There, too, it was so eerily quiet they could have heard a pin drop. Increasingly assaulted by a stench of alcohol and decay, they made their way past the laundry room and a few storage spaces to the main area filled with splintered pieces of furniture and a row of crates of red wine. In the middle, there stood a solid table of unusual length, largely covered with sundry papers, and, slumped over the end of it, they found the principal object of their search.

CHAPTER

It was Agnes, her head resting on a bulky notebook and her right arm stretched out toward an overturned bottle. Inspector Stein who had never made her acquaintance saw, lying before him, an emaciated woman with thin grayish-brown hair and pinched features, her pale-blue eyes staring at the pen that had fallen from her left hand. His first impression had been that she had drifted off to sleep after a night of drinking but a second look told him otherwise. Agnes was dead.

After her body had been taken away, the team began to examine her home for evidence. The richest and most rewarding source of information turned out to be the notebook in which Agnes was apparently writing when she died. Made up of tattered and dog-eared pages, it had served her as a crude and simple diary. In it, she had recorded the disintegration of her marriage, her growing anxiety over her children's slide into criminality, and their going away which she perceived as desertion. She also dwelled on the deep hurt she felt when her speeches were banned, for which she blamed Olga alone and vowed bitter revenge. Olga had ruined her life and, for that, Agnes showered her with an amazing repertory of vile curses.

Agnes had actually considered killing Olga for what she had done to her but came to believe that such a death would be too quick and too merciful by far. She needed to strike Olga where it would hurt the most, which meant dealing a lethal blow to her pride and reputation, and she knew just how to do it: frame her for despicable crimes that would result in the worst kind of humiliation she could imagine—being branded as a monster and incarcerated for the rest of her days.

To get some ideas of how to accomplish this, Agnes had to follow Olga around the park. Since remaining unobtrusive by threading in and out of the shrubbery had become a way of life for Agnes while she was making her home among the trees, trailing Olga without being noticed should be easy, she told herself, and it was. But killing someone other than Olga did not occur to her until she had observed Olga's favorite pastime of loudly and aggressively arguing with other pet owners. What if Olga went too far and killed them, she pondered. What if I did it for her, and she would get the blame, Agnes was thinking prior to her deciding on her course of action.

How could she do it, she was wondering when, to her deep satisfaction, she remembered Olga's interest in poisonous plants, the most common and potentially deadliest of which, to her knowledge, was the castor-oil plant featured in most city flower beds. "Perfect," she must have exclaimed, rubbing her hands together in anticipation. She had come up with the ideal method to implement her plan.

Three full pages of the diary were dedicated to Agnes's experimentation with the plant as a toxic agent and notes on ricin in particular. At one point, she evidently ground the seeds and mixed them with melted chocolate or pungent preserves such as ginger to cover up the taste of the noxious particles. How she incorporated these mixtures into treats, and whether or not she went so far as to isolate ricin in its pure form, was not made clear in the text.

What Agnes did say, however, was that she followed the victims of Olga's tongue-lashings, commiserated with them, commented on Olga's ghastly behavior, and offered them one of her ricin-laced confections to compensate for Olga's malice. Her comforting words were usually welcome although, to Agnes's disappointment, her sweets were often turned down with regrets or apologies.

The few people who did accept Agnes's treats initially were not affected, at least not seriously. At worst they might have endured abdominal pain, diarrhea, and vomiting but, to Agnes's consternation, always returned to the park. So Agnes incrementally increased the dose of her special ingredient until Bertha's death confirmed that she had reached the correct amount she needed to take a life.

As the officers were skimming page after page of the voluminous diary, they noticed that Agnes's handwriting had declined progressively, conceivably due to advancing alcoholism and overwhelming emotional involvement on her part. At times it became almost illegible, resembling her writing in the two notes she had delivered to the station. So perhaps it had not been disguised at all but had simply deteriorated. Just like the notes, many diary pages were torn and crumpled. There were comments scrawled all over, most of them consisting of foul language, and toward the end, one line kept reappearing: "I want to die," Agnes wrote over and over again.

On the last page, she expressed her utter frustration with the police department. "I give up," she declared when it became obvious to her that, even after her second note had been received, Olga was still enjoying her freedom when she should have been arrested immediately. Her final statement was "I want to die," followed by a row of shaky exclamation marks trailing off onto the table.

Agnes's guilt notwithstanding, Inspector Stein and his colleagues were profoundly shaken by her utter wretchedness and tragic demise. They felt tremendous evil but also immense suffering. The post-mortem would have to determine the cause of death although the officers agreed that most likely it had come about as the result of starvation and years of alcohol abuse and may have been compounded by a broken heart.

The diary provided all the evidence the authorities needed to build a strong case against Agnes. Knowing that proof of the presence of ricin in the home would bolster it even further, the officers searched for it throughout the residence. Failing to find any upstairs or in the basement, they returned to the kitchen where, in a cabinet, they located a small tin of speckled castor beans, a little container of what appeared to be ground seeds, and two larger jars labeled "edible" and "inedible," respectively, that were both empty. It looked like Agnes might have been selective in her choice of victims, not wanting to kill at random. No one would ever know for certain, and although there was a confession and plenty of corroboration, there would be neither trial nor conviction. Agnes had carried out her own punishment.

The investigation was closed. Inspector Stein had notified both Bertha's and Lilly's families and Oskar's ex-wife that the perpetrator had been identified, who it had been, and how she had died. He had also made a courtesy call on Olga to compliment her on her astuteness and thank her again for her assistance. The public read about it on the front page of the paper a few days later. No one was happy about the outcome although the people who walked their dogs in the park were relieved, and Olga, no longer a suspect, proudly announced to all she encountered that it was she who had solved the case.

Agnes was quietly laid to rest in an old churchyard on the outskirts of town. There was no obituary announcing her funeral. It was a subdued affair attended only by Philipp, Simon, and Sister Maria, each offering a prayer for the peace of Agnes's soul.

Agnes's home which had been off-limits to Philipp during the investigation following her death was returned to him in due time. It was still his property although the profound anguish he associated with it kept him away. He did not want to set foot in it ever again. But he did want to make sure that something good would come of the tragedy. At great expense to himself, he had both house and grounds thoroughly cleaned up, the debris hauled away, the floors, windows, walls, doors, and light fixtures replaced or repaired, as well as a fresh coat of paint applied throughout. Once the property looked like new again inside and out, he sold it at a good price and divided the proceeds among the families of Bertha and Lilly and, in Oscar's case, a frontotemporal dementia research facility.

CHAPTER

Another winter went by, turning the neighbors' breath, once again, into icy droplets of mist. They could not wait for the sun to melt the snow that had spread its desolation over the park. And there was something else they were equally looking forward to: the realization of a relatively small-scale but ambitious project announced by the city. It would involve converting a section of the lawn close to the angel fountain into a special flower bed meant to introduce new plants and illustrate the advantages of organic gardening. Classes were scheduled to be held on this topic once a week, and additional benches were to be installed in the area for anyone who wished to participate or just sit in the sun, relaxing and enjoying the view.

Work on the project began in the spring. City gardeners dug up the ground and removed the grass. They brought in fresh soil and compost, spread them out evenly, and placed an attractive granite curb around the outer boundary. To vary the surface, they created little hills and valleys and added some white, yellow, and orange-reddish sand here and there. The plants were delivered by truck, then loaded on wheelbarrows and distributed over the flower bed in an interesting mix of colors, textures, and shapes so that a clump of blossoms would alternate with a single stem of ornamental grass, blue with pink, and orange with turquoise or lime green.

When it was finished, and the plants had had time to grow and bloom, it was beautiful. People came to admire it, and the bees loved it. It was a corner of paradise that could lift heavy hearts, soothe frayed nerves, and delight the eyes. It became Hilde and Sylvia's favorite destination. There they spent many an evening, listening to the sweet songs of the blackbirds and marveling at the lovely flowers in front of them. Amazed how its magic was able to restore their well-being after long tiring days, they invited Zora and Adi, Hans and Frieda, as well as Olga and Sister Maria to experience it with them. They all came when they could—all but Olga.

It seemed strange. Olga was the one who loved flowers and always appeared to be eager to improve her gardening skills, and yet she was glaringly absent. What happened, they asked themselves. Has she lost interest? Even if she has, they thought, she could still be there with them and take pleasure in the beauty that surrounded them. It would do her a world of good.

Olga had not lost interest—far from it. She was once again up to her old tricks. Plants, especially rare and striking ones, fascinated her as much as ever, and she still longed to earn a spot in the flower show. She could now get all the answers she needed from the city botanist who was teaching the classes but could not bear the thought of listening to any more advice, ever. She was tired, tired of working the soil, tired of studying plants, and tired of experimenting. No longer satisfied with just looking at the lovely flowers planted by the city, she wanted to touch and possess them.

Having anyone around would have defeated her purpose. To insure privacy, she was forever waiting in the wings, watching for people to come and go, and whenever no one was close-by, she jumped at her chance. She quickly stepped over the curb, entered the flower bed, cut some plants and pulled others up by their roots. She then hid them in her bag and furtively left the area.

One morning she was not so lucky. She felt excruciating stabs of pain, tripped over the curb, and stumbled a few more steps until she lost her balance and fell face-down on the grass. Struggling for breath, she slipped into unconsciousness. When one of the city gardeners found her, it was too late. Olga was dead.

Next to her on the ground there was a pale-lavender spike of Russian sage. It was obvious where it had come from and that it would have ended up in Olga's bag together with the other plants she had taken, had she lived.

But how had she died, wondered the paramedics when they picked up the body. Unless there was a copycat killer, the likelihood of another poisoning was minimal. In the absence of any signs of violence, they assumed that Olga might have suffered a stroke or heart attack. And they were right, up to a point: After detecting the stinger of a honeybee still anchored in Olga's skin and the swelling it had caused, the medical examiner ruled it a death by cardiac arrest brought on by anaphylactic shock.

When the neighbors found out what had happened to Olga, they were stunned but shed no tears. "It's like nature took revenge on Olga," said Sylvia. "She must have grabbed a flower and gotten hold of a bee along with it." "She should have left other people's plants alone," commented Hilde. "I wonder what will become of her home and belongings now," she added, secretly hoping that, as promised, she would inherit Olga's flat.

Frieda brought up Olga's obituary. "Who is going to write it and have it published," she asked, and it was Hans who suggested that they all sit down and compose it together and then share the cost of putting it in the paper. "We are the ones who knew her best and although she has mentioned relatives, she's had nothing to do with them for years, and we have no idea where they might be. She has no one else. So let's do her this one last favor," he proposed, and everyone agreed.

Olga had been difficult but they bore her no ill-will. They were deeply sorry that she had to die all alone and even sorrier for Fluffy who had lost the only mistress he had ever known. Again, it was Hans who saved the day. "Frieda and I will take him," he assured the others. "We've already talked about it. With our children out of the house, we have plenty of room, and I suspect Fluffy will not only be happy but also the most spoiled little dog in the world."

At the neighbors' request, Sister Maria took charge of the funeral. She would make arrangements for it to be held at the Cemetery of the Church of Peace where Olga would be interred next to her parents and sister. On the appointed day, almost all the residents of Olga's building as well as Zora and Adi turned out to accompany Olga on her last journey.

Olga's coffin was covered with beautiful flowers, and several lovely wreaths had been set up in a semicircle facing the mourners. The service was solemn and dignified. There were no eulogies since Olga had always considered them frivolous although she would have been over the moon, had one of the local luminaries agreed to speak at her funeral. But none of these were in attendance.

CHAPTER

42

The attorney handling Olga's will was Herr Goldfuss, and everyone who expected to inherit anxiously awaited his call. But no call came. For Olga's savings as well as her flat that she had promised to quite a few people in exchange for being always at her beck and call were to go exclusively to a canine charity benefitting abused dogs.

When Hilde learned of Olga's provisions, she felt shamelessly used and utterly disillusioned. Her hopes of finally getting a home of her own were dashed. She was sick at heart. All these years she had been making outfits for Fluffy and helping Olga in other ways as well, and now there would be no reward for any of it. It didn't have to be the flat; it could have been just a small legacy. But nothing at all? She could not believe it. What kind of person would be so cruel as to do this to her? Definitely not someone she should have trusted, she conceded, feeling like a fool to have pinned her hopes on any promise Olga might have made.

These were the thoughts going through Hilde's mind and the minds of all the others, too, to whom Olga had made a similar promise. Like Hilde, they felt exploited but none to the extent that she did. She had done the most for Olga, and Olga's callous lack of gratitude had hit her the hardest. She felt too humiliated and devastated to tell Sylvia about it although she was her best friend and would never have mocked her for being gullible. Hilde could not talk about it to anyone, at least not now. It had been too much of a blow, and she was hurt to the depths of her being.

But Sylvia did not need to be told how Hilde felt. She had seen the sadness in her eyes, had sensed her profound disappointment, and was trying to think of ways to make it up to her, even if only to a small degree. Obviously she could not do anything about her circumstances, financial or personal. Since Hilde already knew that she could count on her support, just reassuring her on that point was not enough. Sylvia wanted to do more. If only I could come up with something special, she reflected.

After a bit of deliberation, it occurred to her that if anyone could help, it would be Bastl and Ulli. She went to their shop, explained her problem to them, and asked them if they could think of a solution. They weighed several options and eventually made a delightful suggestion: Instead of a mask, they would create a big red heart embellished with multicolored paisleys of little beads, shiny sequins, and pieces of glass that Hilde could hang on her wall. It would be a symbol of love, reminding her of the affection her fellow human beings held for her in their hearts every time she looked at it.

Picturing it in her mind, Sylvia was excited. She had a feeling that the idea had already taken shape and come to life in Ulli's and Bastl's imagination and was convinced it would be carried out to perfection. A week later, Bastl and Ulli invited Sylvia and Hilde to their shop, unveiled the heart, and presented it to Hilde "in the name of our small community, and to say we love you." "You have done so much for your patients and neighbors," they continued, "that it's time we showed our appreciation and thanked you for your friendship." In Sylvia's ear, Bastl whispered that it was a gift and that there was no charge.

Overwhelmed by their kindness, the loveliness of the heart, and the sweet thought behind it, Hilde could not hold back her tears. "I love you, too," she sobbed, "and I love the beautiful heart you have made for me. You have no idea what it means to me. I was devastated and now I can laugh again. You have made me so happy. The heart will be my most treasured possession. I will hang it up as soon as I get home, and I will never forget your generosity."

The heart was indeed exquisite, a mosaic of delicate, intricate, and colorful paisleys on a red background, glittering in the light. Both Hilde and Sylvia marveled at its beauty, profusely thanked Bastl and Ulli and said their good-byes, exchanging big hugs with the two men whose good will had so enriched their lives. When Hilde looked back at them, they no longer saw tears but a smile on her face.

CHAPTER

43

I ronically, the flat Olga had duped Hilde into believing she would inherit upon her death did not benefit her intended leg-atee either. For poetic justice prevailed in the end: It turned out that the machinations of the animal charity whom Olga had made the beneficiary of her will had been subject to a lengthy investigation, with the result that its officials were found guilty of fraud, and, before they could profit from Olga's bequest, their assets were seized. The city was granted ownership not only of their local real estate but of all the funds they had raised locally which included one hundred per cent of Olga's endowment. Free to disburse this unexpected windfall as they saw fit, the city fathers chose to spend it on finally updating the small wooden cottages in the community garden occupied by Zora and Adi and a number of other displaced persons for decades.

When the residents found out, they were ecstatic. They would finally have adequate bathroom facilities and, if they were lucky enough, perhaps also an additional storage space or two. Overjoyed by the city's decision, Zora and Adi danced around Zora's garden while Max excitedly fluttered about them, cawing for attention. The city's beneficence did not stop there, however. Along with the struc-tural and sanitary improvements to the little homes, all occupants would also receive stipends to compensate them for the years the cottages had been considered below acceptable standards.

Zora and Adi could not wait to share their joy with their favorite people and immediately put their heads together to come up with the best celebration ever. And when their friends insisted on helping them to plan the big event, preparing for it became a cheerful community effort. Small tables and chairs appeared in Zora's yard, Chinese lanterns turned up hanging from the branches of her trees, and colorful garlands materialized along the railings of her porch.

On the morning of the festivities, Zora and Adi observed their friends scurrying in and out, leaving on Zora's steps all sorts of mouth-watering dishes, bottles of mineral water and wine, and vases filled with beautiful flowers. Hans and Frieda were the only ones who managed to slip in unnoticed. They quickly and quietly set the tables with checkered cotton tablecloths and plates, silverware, and napkins from their own kitchen and then tiptoed out, softly closing the gate.

When Zora and Adi peeked through Zora's lace curtains again, everything seemed ready for the party. Nothing was left to be done, which did not bother the easy-going Adi but did not seem fair to Zora. "Adi," she said to him, "it's our celebration and, while our friends have done all the work, I did not lift a finger. Don't you think we should have contributed a little, too?" "Don't worry, Zora," Adi replied. "Just be happy that we have friends who care enough to have lined up such a wonderful surprise and had fun doing it. Besides, it's not as if you haven't done your share. I saw the tons of cookies you baked and all the desserts in your fridge," he added, making Zora smile. What Adi had missed, however, were the fragrant candles that Zora now ran out to place on the tables.

It was a golden Indian summer afternoon when the guests arrived. The red, orange, and yellow leaves were shining in the sun, and the birds were celebrating the mild air with their songs. Colorful berries and interesting seed pods as well as patches of hearty flowers that had survived the cold of recent nights filled Zora's yard. Serenity, peace, and harmony reigned.

Zora and Adi stood on Zora's steps, beaming with pleasure as they welcomed Sylvia and Hilde, Hans and Frieda, and Bastl and

Ulli who had brought along a radiant Liesl. Sister Maria was the next to arrive, accompanied by Mimi, a little girl from the orphanage who desperately needed some joy in her life. And finally, a special guest made an appearance, someone only the hosts had expected but all were pleased to see: It was Inspector Stein carrying his guitar.

Once all were seated, Max swooped in and hopped from table to table to greet each and every one with a friendly "hello," much to Mimi's delight. They then enjoyed an excellent meal and lively conversation, remembering to raise their glasses to Olga who was ultimately yet unwittingly responsible for their deep contentment. They felt so comfortable in one another's company that, while they were happily chatting, the hours slipped by almost unnoticed. As the sun was slowly going down, its light was replaced by the burning candles on the tables and the Chinese lanterns in the trees, casting a lovely glow over Zora's yard.

After some prodding, Mimi sang a funny little ditty which earned her a standing ovation. And suddenly everyone was singing, accompanied by Ulli's harmonica and the inspector's guitar. Punctuated by a few instrumentals, one song gave rise to another until, when the music was winding down, Zora and Adi made a surprise announcement: They had booked a trip to Saintes-Maries-de-la-Mer to fulfill Zora's life-long dream and give her an opportunity to share her Gypsy heritage and traditions with her best friend. Loud applause followed and eventually gave way to a beautiful melody sung by Zora alone, her singular and spell-binding voice ringing out over the park.

ABOUT THE AUTHOR

Rosina Anderson was born in Bavaria and now lives in Albuquerque. She has taught modern languages at US universities, held the position of scientific-technical assistant at a psychiatric research institute in Munich, and worked as an interpreter in the ER of a California hospital. She enjoys traveling and painting.